CACTUS
CRADLE

A TEXAS WINE TRAIL SERIES

≫ BOOK 3 ≪

CACTUS CRADLE

A TEXAS WINE TRAIL SERIES

⇒ BOOK 3 ⇐

Heather Renée May

MAYDAY PUBLISHING LTD

For special bulk discounts, or to arrange for the author to attend your live event, please visit the author's website, or address correspondence to: www.heatherreneemay.com

MayDay Publishing Ltd. Co.
2028 E Ben White Blvd #240-5666
Austin, TX 78741

Cover & Interior Design by the Book Cover Whisperer:
OpenBookDesign.biz

Chapter Illustrations by Victoria Horner
Editing & Proofreading through NYBookEditors
Line/Structural Editing by Megan McKeever
Copyediting by Robert J.
Headshot/Bio Photos by Abraham Rowe Photography

Library of Congress Control Number: 2024915996

978-1-7377193-5-9 Paperback
978-1-7377193-6-6 eBook

Manufactured in the United States of America

Printing & Distribution by

KC Book Mfg | IngramSpark | Kindle Direct Publishing

FIRST EDITION

This book is dedicated to my biggest critic and fan, Jimmy Farrell, Sr. "One more, no more!" (RIP 1938-2024).

⇉ Foreword ⇇

This book contains fictional characters, and any resemblance to persons living or dead is purely coincidental. However, the places in this book were real at the time of writing. This book is not meant to be an exhaustive list of wineries or businesses in Fredericksburg and the Texas Hill Country. Rather, the author encourages readers to come visit this beautiful and unique Texas wine country and experience it firsthand. At the back of this book is a listing of all locations highlighted for reference.

Further, this book is not meant to be used as a guide for RV life. There are plenty of resources that are much more comprehensive than this that the author encourages you to explore

"When the bough breaks, the cradle will fall..."

⇛ One ⇚

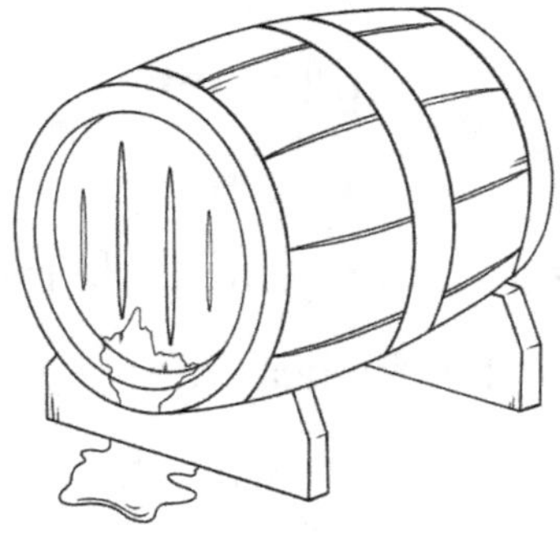

Aflash of light illuminated the skyline of the Hill Country, then a crescendo of thunder came barreling across the land like a train on an invisible track. The ground reverberated with the weight of the violence, seeming to absorb the magnitude in an unspoken pact. A steady staccato of rain drops came down and blanketed the terrain, quickly filling the deep dried cracks from the previous season's drought.

Another flash of lightning contrasted the

dark contours of the Slate Theory Winery, sitting quietly up on the hill. The thunder came soon after, impatient with a commanding melody to offset the unrelenting rhythmic rain. Water filled every possible opening and rushed between the vines to pool along Highway 290.

Within the sturdy cement walls of the winery, you could hardly hear the storm's fury outside. Metal stairs led down to the secure barrel room. Rows and rows of oak barrels stacked high covered the expanse of the underground cellar. The cave was empty, the soft glow of LED lights exposed the rough contours of the archways. Behind a single row of barrels stacked double high, a shadow moved. There was a faint sound of a drill. Then silence.

———

KATE WOKE UP GROGGY FROM the overnight storm. She stretched inside her Airstream trailer and looked out the window to see that the deluge of rain had power-washed the dusty pavement of the RV park, leaving behind haphazard fallen branches. Birds were emerging from their shelter tweeting in relief as they rushed between the live oak trees. Kate was always amazed at how loud the rain could be inside her trailer. The incessant pounding overnight made it tough to sleep. She had finally dozed off before sunrise when the lightning and rumble of thunder moved east.

Setting water to boil for her morning coffee, she looked at her phone and saw a text message from Zach: *Hope you managed ok last night? Sure missed having you here. XO*

Kate sighed deeply as the water began to percolate in the pot. As happy as she was being closer to Zach now that he had a home in the Hill Country, she still loved her time alone in her trailer in Spicewood. It was the only way she felt she could really tap into her creative vision for her writing. She had just finished edits on her fourth novel and had a good feeling about it.

Two years ago, Zach and Kate had their first fateful meeting on the Texas wine trail at Texas Heritage Vineyard. Zach was a doctor from the northeast scouting for a winery to invest in and they decided to pair up to do some tastings.

Kate took a sip of her coffee as she thought back to how difficult that time had been for her. She had just begun the process of legally separating from her now ex-husband, and was struggling with writer's block. Her marriage had become toxic, and just the thought of that dark time sent a shiver down her spine. That week with Zach had been a beacon of hope.

Kate watched a bright red cardinal flit past her window and duck under the foliage of a live oak next to her trailer. She remembered back then, how Zach had to leave suddenly. At the time, she wasn't sure she would ever see him again. But fate had a different plan.

Last year, they ran into each other at Pontotoc Vineyards in downtown Fredericksburg, and picked right back up like no time had passed. He was opening a tasting room on Main Street, and his daughter Chloe had moved to Austin to attend the University of Texas.

She topped off her coffee and lightened it with oat milk. Sitting down at her tiny dinette table, she looked out onto the peaceful park, amazed at how everything turned out. She loved living full-time in her trailer, and just a forty-five-minute drive to Zach and his tasting room. It all seemed almost too good to be true.

Putting her coffee mug down, Kate picked up her phone and finally replied: *What a storm. It was so loud! All is fine here. Miss you too. xxo*

Two

It was Thursday morning and traffic in downtown Fredericksburg was just picking up. Chloe pulled her Prius up in front of her dad's tasting room, Winsome Winery. She felt so much pride every time she stepped up to those bold letters etched in the glass. It was early June, and her summer break at UT. She had insisted on helping her dad at the tasting room as the tourist traffic swelled in summer and seemed to only increase every year.

She stepped inside and instantly smelled the scent of Mexican pine and leather furniture that was familiar and comforting. "Dad, I'm here!" she said as she made her way around the long bar to put her purse and water bottle on the shelf below and began taking the barstools off the bar top and turning them right-side up to place evenly in front of the counter.

Zach came out from the storeroom with a white case of bottles. "Hello, sweetie!" He gave her a kiss on the cheek before putting down the box. "Here's some extra bottles of the Viognier. That's been a big seller so far, and I figure we should be prepared."

Chloe nodded and hummed as she went about her business. She watched some tourists pass by the picture window peering in. Chloe waved to them and mouthed, "Open soon!" as she pointed to the business hours on the door.

Zach turned on the rest of the lights and started pulling the slender bottles out of the box, placing them in the custom cut cubby holes behind the bar. The shelving behind the bar took up the entire expanse of the wall, creating quite an impressive display of bottles. The butcher block counter underneath held rows upon rows of shiny glasses just waiting to be filled.

Chloe turned on the WiFi speaker and started the playlist she had created for the tasting room earlier that year. A combination of acoustic, soul-inspired singer-songwriters with just the right mellow, but high vibe.

"Oh! I meant to tell you, I talked with Lillie today and she gave me the number of that duo you were looking to book," she told Zach.

"Excellent," he said, as he stayed focused on his bottles. "I'd rather have her and Paul, but we have that bachelorette party reservation and I promised them live music."

Chloe nodded and surveyed the room to see what else needed to be done before opening. She went to the back patio and grabbed a broom to sweep off the seats. Turning on the hanging lights, she remembered how beautiful it was when Lillie and Paul had their wedding there, and how she loved capturing the candid moments with her camera.

Lillie was Kate's sister, and she had spent time as a touring musician in France before returning to the States unexpectedly pregnant. Chloe shivered at the thought of having a baby at her age, but Paul ended up coming from France to live with her and a few months after the wedding they had a beautiful baby girl, Emma.

After their breathtaking musical performance at the wedding party, it was agreed that they would be the "house" band at the tasting room. People came from all over to hear Lillie on her violin, with her hauntingly beautiful voice, with Paul backing her up on exquisite guitar.

The instant Chloe met Lillie they bonded. They were just a few years apart in age, and it was like they were cut from the same cloth.

She cherished their friendship and helped watch Emma when she could, although they had gone back to France to visit Paul's parents for a few months.

Coming back into the main tasting room, she went behind the bar next to her father and began putting pouring spouts onto the bottles he was opening.

"How was your trip in?" he asked her.

"Perfect. Not too much traffic at all," Chloe responded, gently nudging a spout in.

"You know, you're always welcome to stay at the house when you're working multiple days in a row," Zach reminded Chloe.

She laughed. "You say that every time, but I like going back to my own place, and it's not like the tasting room stays open that late. Besides, what if Kate comes to stay?"

Chloe had grown very close to Kate, but still felt a bit awkward sharing her father's home with someone else. Kate had definitely won her over with her warm spirit and big heart. Chloe knew it was only a matter of time before they would be tying the knot as well.

"There's plenty of room. And Kate prefers to stay in her trailer most of the time so she can focus on her writing," Zach said as he broke down a box to take back to the storeroom.

Chloe knew that if he had his way, she'd be living with him full-time in Fredericksburg. It's not that Chloe didn't want to spend time with him, but she loved her independence.

"Ready to open?" Chloe sang as she headed to the door.

"Yup. Let's do it!" Zach said, taking the last empty box from the bar into the storeroom. He heard the bell on the door ding as Chloe unlocked it and put a wooden easel outside on the sidewalk announcing Live Music @1pm.

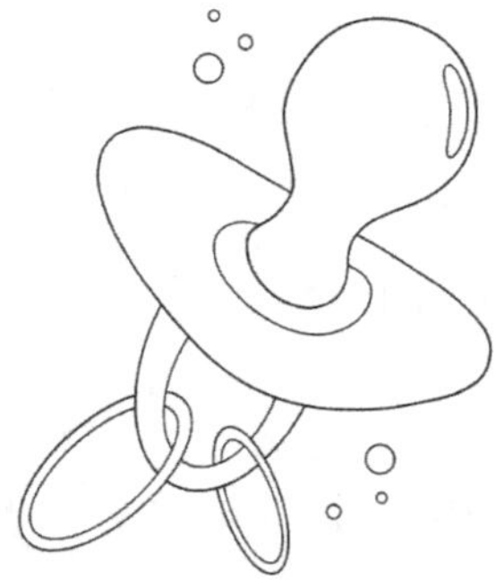

Three

"Kate!" Lillie answered after just a few rings. "Sis! How are you? How's France?" Kate was delighted to hear her voice.

"It's been a fabulous trip so far. I forgot how absolutely beautiful it is here in the summer, with the vines, the flowers, and the food... But, of course, it's nothing compared to the Hill Country!"

Kate laughed. "Oh, you don't have to even

try to compare. I'd love to be in France right now instead of this humidity and heat! How are you and Paul getting along with his parents?"

"Just superbe," Lillie said, playing up a French accent. "They are excellent with Emma, giving us a chance to relax and enjoy each other again. In fact, we've taken to napping during the day before dinner and I'm starting to feel human again!"

Kate loved hearing her joy over the line. She had been a bit concerned how Paul's parents would take the news of him having a child with an American. His family was deeply entrenched in the wine business in Burgundy, and as proud to be French as any Texan flying the Lone Star flag.

"Ah, that's fabulous," Kate said, and meant it. "I miss having you here, but this is exactly what you need. Both of you."

"Thanks, Sis," Lillie said. "So, how are

things with your book? With Zach? The winery? Chloe?"

"Ah! One question at a time!" Kate laughed, and then quickly filled her in on the news.

"I'm glad you've made progress with your book," Lillie said. "Tell me, how do you feel about it?"

"The book? I feel like this one is a bit different somehow." Kate paused, trying to put it into words. "I think this one is going to be a game changer."

"Ah!" Lillie squealed. "I think you're right. You know they say it takes a few books to really find your voice as an author."

"Yes, much like wine, I think that my writing is beginning to age at just the right time," Kate said.

They finished catching up on Paul and all the other news across the pond, and then agreed to talk in another week.

Kate stood up from her dinette to stretch her legs. She watched a neighbor walking her white dog with a short stubby tail outside and gave a wave of hello as they passed.

Her phone buzzed and she looked down to see a message from Zach: *Breakfast tomorrow? Usual time & place?*

Her stomach growled just thinking about it. She responded, *You bet. See you tomorrow xo*

Then, she saw a heart appear on her response and smiled.

She poured herself a tall glass of water and sat back down, opened her laptop, and got back to work on her novel.

⇾ Four ⇽

It was early in the morning when Kate pulled up to grab a coveted parking spot at The Sunset Grill in Fredericksburg, her favorite breakfast joint. She was meeting Zach before he had to open the tasting room. She could almost taste the "Sunsetter Benedict" she was going to order.

She saw Zach from the front door and he stood up, smiling as she came closer. He gave her a big hug and she relaxed into his arms for a moment before giving him a sweet kiss and sitting down opposite him.

"I missed those lips," he said to her as he put his napkin back into his lap.

"I was just thinking the same thing." Kate smiled as the waitress came up and poured her coffee.

After giving their order, Zach focused back on Kate. "Dennis said he wanted to join us if that's okay?"

"Oh, sure!" Kate said. She hadn't seen Zach's partner in a while due to being busy with the book. Dennis was also more of a vineyard guy, preferring the vines or the production facility to the tasting room.

Before she could ask how he was doing, she saw a large figure come through the doorway.

"Pardon me for being late," Dennis said politely with his signature Texas twang. He gave Kate a quick hug, and then shook Zach's hand, taking off his cowboy hat and placing it in the other empty seat.

"It's good to see you," Kate said.

"Good to be seen," he chuckled, and then quickly added his order as the waitress poured him a black coffee.

"So, what's going on, Dennis? How are things looking at the vineyard?" Zach asked before taking a sip from of his mug.

"Well, sorry to bring up bad news, but there's been some rumblings around town," Dennis said grimly.

Kate side-eyed Zach and listened as he continued.

He cleared his throat. "Some of the growers are seeing strange things happening with their vines this season."

Zach sat up straighter. "Really? Like what?"

"Well, seems some hail netting has been cut, and there's more rodent infestations than usual."

"Huh, that's strange. Do you think it's just a random coincidence?" Zach asked.

"Hard to say. Maybe separately. But all together, it doesn't add up." His face was set in a grim line.

"But what about your vines?" Kate interjected.

Dennis patted her hand. "Oh, don't worry, ours are fine right now. I've been vigilant." He turned to Zach. "I just thought you should know." He cleared his throat again and lowered his voice leaning towards them both. "There's talk as well that might point to something else going on."

Kate's eyebrows raised as she looked at Zach and then back to Dennis.

"Seems this all started when the you-know-who moved to town." He shrugged, then leaned back. "Just saying. It's not painting a pretty picture."

Kate sat amazed. She knew who he was

talking about. The Californians who had come to the Hill Country, buying up the available properties and building wineries up and down Highway 290. She remembered their former business partner, Peter, who was from California and was supposed to be the money man behind the Winsome Winery tasting room, but was forced out after he insisted on shipping California juice to Texas to bottle under the guise of Texas wine.

Kate shuddered when she recalled how angry Zach and Dennis had gotten, and how stressful it was to try to get Texas juice to bottle in time to open the tasting room. It added a tremendous expense and threatened to shut down Zach's dreams. Luckily, he was good with the locals, and many of them stepped up to help at the eleventh hour.

"I hate to ask this, but how is Peter's tasting room doing?" Kate sipped her coffee tentatively, knowing that he ended up partnering with someone else bringing international wines to a room on Main Street.

"Harrumph." Dennis sat back in his seat looking like he'd rather be bit by a rattlesnake than talk about him.

"It's no competition with us, and we don't ever see one another," Zach responded.

Dennis leaned forward and eyed Zach. "He's such an oily sucker, I wouldn't put it past him to try anything for more profit."

Zach shook his head. "Dennis, we've talked about this. What happened, happened. And it's good we found out so early. Now we have a good partnership with the other local wineries, and we've made some excellent friends. There's plenty of space in Fredericksburg for all of us."

Dennis grunted just as the food came and Kate was hopeful that the conversation would pause long enough for them to eat in peace.

They finished their breakfast mostly in silence. Dennis asked Kate about her book, Lillie and Paul, and Emma. He had been the officiant at their wedding and had offered them a rental house on his property. It was such a blessing for Kate and Lillie. With an absent father, and their mother succumbing to cancer, his fatherly presence made them both feel like they had a real home there.

"Everyone's doing great, they're loving France." Kate filled them both in on her recent conversation.

The waitress cleared the plates and, before Zach could, Dennis grabbed the check.

"It's on me today." He winked and nodded. "Pleasure seeing you again, Kate." She stood and gave him a hug and peck on the cheek.

"I'll be in touch with you later," Dennis motioned to Zach as he stood and they shook hands again.

As he left, Kate and Zach looked at one another and for a moment, she thought she saw concern flash in his eyes.

"I'm not worried," he said, as if reading her thoughts. "You know how people talk. And Dennis is biased. I wish he would be a bit more open, but that's his line in the sand."

"Nobody likes change, I guess," Kate ventured.

"Especially not in a place with strong generational ties to the land. I totally get where Dennis is coming from, but I also think that he could be more open-minded about sharing the land as well."

He walked Kate out to her car and then pulled her towards him. She breathed in his trademark aftershave deeply. Looking up at him, their faces were close together and he placed his firm lips against hers, giving her a kiss that sent shivers down her spine.

He then pulled away slightly and brushed her cheek. "Let's do a sleepover soon?"

She blushed, nodding. The blood in her lips slowly returned to her head.

He waved goodbye as she got into her car. Seeing him in her rearview, she touched her lips with her fingers and marveled again at how such a fine man could be in love with her.

⇛   **Five**   ⇚

Chloe had driven to town early to stop by Walmart and pick up some supplies for the tasting room. She wanted to create a collage of photos of their wine club members that they could hang on the wall to commemorate the tasting room's first anniversary.

Standing in the frame aisle debating whether to go with wood or metal, she saw a flash of red out of the corner of her eye and turned to see the most drop dead gorgeous guy pause between aisles and then continue out of sight. He was tall, fit, with a luxurious crop of long curly red hair that hung over his forehead, making her want to swoon. He looked so out of place there, like a surfer in ranch country.

She laughed at herself and then headed up to the checkout. Standing in line waiting for a self-checkout to open, he came up behind her. She turned around and smiled.

He grinned at her, and she felt her cheeks flush so she quickly headed to an open register.

She was aware of him the entire time she was scanning her purchase. It looked like he was buying some paint brushes and some sort of sealant. She continued checking out, and then grabbed her receipt as she picked up her frames and headed towards the sliding doors.

"Hey." She heard a voice behind her. She turned to look up into his deep green eyes.

"Um, hi," she stammered.

"I'm new here, do you know where to get the best caramel latte?" he asked, his face open and bright.

"Um, yeah, I kind of figured you're not from around here, being that you aren't wearing cowboy boots or a hat." She giggled.

He looked down at his Roxy t-shirt and shrugged. "Guilty."

"There's a great place called Sunday Supply that's not far from here. They have the best coffee," Chloe said, tucking a strand of her blond hair behind her ear.

"Awesome. Thanks." He grinned again at her, then asked, "If you aren't busy, do you want to join me? My treat."

Chloe's heart took a leap. She looked down at her Apple watch and saw it was an hour before she needed to open the tasting room. "Sure. I can get a quick one." She nodded to her car. "I'll meet you there?"

"Sweet." He smiled wide and she caught his

perfectly straight teeth. Sticking his hand out he said, "I'm Chase."

She took his hand. "Chloe."

She headed to her Prius and after placing the frames inside, closed the door and nearly squealed in delight. "Oh my gosh, he is SO cute!" She laughed at herself and tried to keep it together.

She texted her dad: *Going to be a few minutes late for opening if that's ok?*

He responded immediately: *No prob*

AFTER FINDING A SPOT ON the street, Chloe walked around to the front of Sunday Supply and saw Chase standing there, his back to her, as he was taking in the scenery.

"Hey!" she said, a bit too brightly.

He turned around and flashed his million-dollar grin. "This place is super cool." He stepped up to open the door for her and she smiled and walked in.

They ordered their coffee at the counter and then found a cute antique table in the back for privacy near a window that overlooked the garden. Beautiful butterflies flitted about the colorful flowers outside as they settled into their seats.

"I hope this isn't too weird?" he asked as he leaned back in his seat, his long legs straddling the table legs.

"Oh, no." She grinned. "I doubt murderers drink caramel lattes."

They both laughed, and she noticed how comfortable she was with him, once she got past the initial flush of attraction.

"Where are you from?" Chloe asked him.

"California." he replied. He heard their names and got up to fetch their coffee.

When he came back, Chloe accepted her

coffee graciously. "I figured as much with your hair and clothes. You look like a surfer."

He took a sip. "Oh yeah, I love to catch some waves. I grew up in Malibu, but moved to LA for school."

"Oh, which school?"

"USC. Go Trojans!" He laughed, and took another sip before asking, "What about you? Are you from here?"

Chloe shook her head, "No, I'm from Boston. But I go to UT in Austin now. I'm just here helping my dad with his tasting room for the summer."

"Dude. I am transferring to UT in fall!" he exclaimed. "It's like our meeting was meant to be."

They both grinned and toasted with their paper coffee cups. Chloe had a strange feeling that she would know Chase for a long time.

"I'm also here helping my dad. He's a

partner in a tasting room on Main Street," Chase explained.

"Oh? Which one?" Chloe couldn't get enough of his eyes.

"All Points Between," he said, taking a long sip.

"Oh." Chloe instantly regretted having asked.

"Do you know it?"

"Um, is your dad named Peter?" Chloe was tentative.

"Yeah! Geez, this is a small town." He laughed.

"Oh, no," Chloe said, and watched the smile on his face disappear.

"Why? What?" he begged.

Chloe fingered her cup, "Well, you see, I think he and my dad used to be business partners, and they had a falling out." She looked up at him. "It was *bad*."

He leaned back in his chair. "Damn. You

know, I don't know anything about my dad's business. He keeps everything to himself."

Chloe frowned. "Yeah, I don't think we can hang out."

"Wait, what? Seriously? That's crazy," he said. "I like you!"

She blushed at how open he was and felt torn. "Thanks, but if my dad found out, I don't think it would go well at all."

He held her stare for a moment, then looked out the window to watch folks entering the Hill & Vine for lunch.

Turning back to her, he was resolute. "Look, that's their business. We're gonna be buds at UT, and I don't know anyone else here to talk to." He paused and leaned forward. "How about we just keep it a summer secret?"

Chloe couldn't resist his charm, nor the lock of red hair that seemed to hang constantly across his tanned forehead.

"Okay, as long as you don't say anything, I won't." She grinned and held out her pinkie.

He locked his pinkie in hers and they swore on it.

The phone buzzed against the metal dinette table. Kate rushed to wrap herself in a towel and stepped out of her shower to see who it was: Caroline.

Caroline was Kate's ride or die friend from Pensacola. She had been by Kate's side through her marriage and divorce, and she had become a sort of second mother to her and Lillie when their mother passed.

"Hang on! I just got out of the shower!"

Kate called as she toweled off the excess water and then made her way back to the dinette to settle in.

"Helloooo! It's just your *favorite* friend calling because you are too busy living a perfect life to call me back." Caroline's drawl was all out.

Kate laughed. "Yes, yes. I know, I'm sorry. It's just been a bit hectic getting the final changes back to my editor." She paused to take a breath. "How are you?"

"Oh, lawd. The usual. Laundry, cleaning, cooking, nagging. Rinse. Repeat," Caroline said. "I'm ready for a vacation."

Kate laughed. "Well, you know, you can always come here?"

"Don't tempt me! Tell me, have you talked with Lillie? How's baby Emma?"

"We caught up the other day. They are having a fabulous time getting pampered in Burgundy. Martine and Didier have been watching Emma so Lillie and Paul can catch up on much needed sleep."

"Oh, fabulous, darlin'! Imagine spending a whole summer in France?" Caroline mused. "Maybe you need to write a book over there, and you need your dear friend to join you?"

"Now, that's a great idea!" Kate laughed. "But, who would pay all my bills?"

Caroline was quick to reply, "Well, you'll be famous soon, no doubt after this next book. Any news?"

"I sent the final draft last week and Margaret said something about fast-tracking it. I'm just waiting to hear what that means exactly." Margaret was Kate's New York literary agent, from Kate's first major success, to a flop, and then back on the *New York Times* best seller list. Kate was grateful for her expertise and their friendship over the years.

"Of course, I trust her completely, but I am curious what she has up her sleeve," Kate mused.

Caroline hummed in agreement and then got to her main point. "Now, tell me how Dr. Wine is doing?"

Kate blushed. "He's good. Chloe has been helping him out in the tasting room for the summer, and they're getting ready to harvest their first merlot grapes."

"Ooh! Maybe I should come visit then? Help out with harvest?" Caroline asked.

"That would be fabulous! We won't know until right before though. So, we can't really plan ahead, but they said sometime at the end of July or beginning of August," Kate said.

"Oh, good. During the hottest part of the season. Fantastic," Caroline replied, her words laced with sarcasm. "Well, I'll see what I can work out on my end."

"I'd love to have you out here again. Maybe you can bring Rob this time?" Kate asked.

There was just a hint of delay in Caroline's response. "Maybe. Well, I'd better be going.

Keep me posted once you hear about your release date!"

They hung up and Kate wondered about Caroline's hesitation when she brought up Rob joining her. Something about it made her question whether there was more to it. She shrugged it off, as Caroline and Rob had always been the power couple, throwing the best dinner parties in Pensacola, and were also model parents. Kate had always thought if she were to get married again, she'd want a marriage like theirs.

She finished towel drying her auburn hair and then began tidying up her trailer. Kate didn't know how much free time she'd have before the book tour spun up, so she wanted to make the most of it. She was excited and anxious about this fourth release. Her last book made the *New York Times* bestseller list, and she wondered if this one would do as well.

She also needed to start noodling her next story. She had a journal where she kept her ideas, things she wanted to research, plots, characters, bits and pieces that may or may not make it into a book. She pulled out that journal and began thumbing through it for inspiration. This was one of her favorite activities—she would add images from magazines, words, phrases, and other notes, like scrapbooking. She flipped the pages and let her imagination carry her away.

KATE GOT UP FROM HER table, had a nice long stretch, and then looked at her clock. 2 pm. She was feeling restless after sitting so long, and her mind was full of all the ideas from her journal. A drive would be the perfect way to let her subconscious sort all the images and ideas. She grabbed her keys and water bottle, and then headed to her Durango.

She had driven the route from Spicewood to Fredericksburg so many times it felt like a habit. Practically on autopilot, she could relax and just coast along. The familiar signs and road markers along the way felt comforting. Even though Kate was technically living in a mobile trailer, she still felt roots in these dusty hills. This place had been good to her for the past few years, and she was grateful for the sense of belonging.

She drove through Main Street in Johnson City, going past the historic town square, then winding her way around until she turned onto Hwy 290. Soon after, she saw the terrain change with more vineyards lined up one after another. She saw new signs and realized that in the time since she had driven this road a week ago, another new winery had opened up. It was surprising to see just how many wineries had cropped up, crowding next to the older, more established ones.

She continued on and saw the signs for Slate Theory Winery. That winery started the previous year and boasted one of the largest multi-million-dollar barrel rooms. It was essentially a cave deep below the ground, and one of the most coveted places for tastings. It was situated next to Grape Creek Vineyards and Heath Sparkling Wines. Kate smiled at the memories of her and Zach doing tastings at Heath years earlier. She remembered the precious older couple they met who were celebrating their 50th wedding anniversary, and how Zach had fibbed and told them they had been together five years, when they had only met a few days before.

She slowed down as a Ram merged in front of her. Funny, she thought, how she and Zach had been so comfortable right from the start. The way everything had worked would be hard to not believe in fate. She looked down at her naked ring finger perched on the steering wheel and wondered if she would ever again be married. She honestly couldn't say whether or not she'd want to, even with Zach being so seemingly perfect.

There was still something she couldn't quite trust about marriage. About partnership. With everything she'd been through with her ex-husband, she was just so glad to be independent and happy. She would never have achieved success with her books had she stayed with him—he was just too needy and jealous.

She sped up again and watched the other buildings and vines drift past. She liked things just as they were. She hoped that would be enough for Zach as well.

She saw a huge white estate up ahead, like a compound. Arch Ray Resort. An RV resort *and* a winery? Kate shook her head at the enormity of it. She couldn't tell how many acres, but it was clearly one of the largest parcels of land along 290. Construction was still underway for the winery, but she saw there was an amphitheater in back. The RV resort next door was situated on the Pedernales River and had more than 75 hookups.

Unbelievable. Just when she thought there wasn't any more space, yet another winery popped up.

Kate was strolling along Main Street when she saw the sign for All Points Between tasting room. She realized this was the place Peter and his new partners from California had opened. Peeking through the window as she walked by, she saw a tall young man with red hair packaging up two bottles of wine as he talked to a couple. She saw shelves of bottles with signs from different regions all over the world. She quickly continued past hoping not to run into Peter.

Further down, she found herself in front of her favorite tasting room: Winsome Winery.

She could see Zach pouring a tasting of some white wine for an older couple, probably the Viognier. She loved watching him at work. He was so handsome and charming. His work with patients when he had his practice in the Northeast clearly set him up to do well with customers in the tasting room. He was patient, knowledgeable, and really enjoyed being around people.

She stepped inside the door and caught his eye mid-pour. He winked at her and nodded before finishing the tasting notes for the couple. Chloe was cleaning up a table and gave Kate a hug while delicately balancing two long stemmed wine glasses. "Hello, stranger!"

"Hi, Chloe! How's your summer so far?"

Kate's heart warmed as she drew back from her embrace.

Chloe bustled around the counter to unload the glasses. "Oh, you know, I have my hands full with this guy here." She rolled her eyes towards her father and laughed. "But seriously, it's been super fun. I've met so many cool people and have learned so much."

Kate thought about how much Chloe reminded her of her sister Lillie. She had grown fond of Chloe, she had a wonderful perspective on life—cheerful and curious.

"Well, after last summer in Paris, I'd imagine this to be anticlimactic?" Kate asked.

"Oh my gosh, last summer was amazing, and honestly I'm still working on picking out my favorite photos to frame." Chloe grinned at her and pointed to the wall. "I finally got a few up, but have also been working on these: a collage of photographs of our wine club members for our one year anniversary!"

Kate walked over and saw a gorgeous shot of an antique Paris Metro sign. The entire photo was in black and white, except for the red background of the sign. "Chloe, I love this one! You have a great eye and way of highlighting specific details." She turned to her. "I hope you can make me a small one to put in my trailer?"

Chloe blushed. "I think I have the perfect one for you—give me a few more weeks to get it touched up."

Kate moved closer to the large poster frames on the wall and delighted in seeing all the happy members. These folks had become part of the Winsome family, and she enjoyed getting together with everyone at the pickup parties.

"I love these. Great idea." Kate turned around just as Zach came up to them.

"This is a surprise!" He smiled and pulled Kate in for a warm embrace.

She looked up at him and gave him a sweet

kiss. "Well, now that my manuscript is done, I'm trying to take advantage of my extra time."

Just then some customers came in the door and Chloe whisked off to greet them.

"Well, I love seeing you anytime." Zach warmed her shoulder with his hands. "Do you want to grab dinner later?"

Kate nodded. "Absolutely. I was thinking we could try going to that new Italian restaurant that opened up?"

"Alla Campagna?"

"Yes, that's the one!" Kate said. "Although, they might not have space. I've heard it's hard to get reservations?"

He winked at her. "I'll make a call. Would you like a glass in the meantime?"

She followed him up to the bar and chose a stool at the end closer to him. "How about that red blend I tried last time?"

He nodded, and placed an empty glass in front of her, turned around gracefully to grab the bottle and then gave her a generous pour. The luscious red slid around the sides of the glass and Kate could hardly wait to take a sip.

He pushed the glass gently towards her. "Enjoy!"

———

AFTER LOCKING UP THE DOOR to the tasting room, and saying goodbye to Chloe, Zach and Kate walked up Main Street towards Alla Campagna. Zach reached for her hand, and Kate reveled in the intimate gesture. She realized that it had been some time since they had strolled like this in downtown Fredericksburg. It felt good.

"Seemed like a good day?" Kate asked him.

Zach nodded. "It was. In fact, I think that we've outpaced our sales this time last year. Of course, that was our first season. But our wine club keeps growing too."

"That's so exciting!" Kate squeezed his hand.

"I just love these white half-curtains," Kate said as they approached the restaurant. "Makes it seem very European."

Zach agreed and then opened the front door for her to step inside. She was greeted instantly by the delicious smells of tomato, spices, and artisanal dough. Kate's stomach growled and she peered at the food already plated on tables to get a sneak peek at her menu options.

Zach motioned her to the bar. "I hope you don't mind sitting at the bar tonight? They didn't have an opening for a table."

"Oh, of course not," Kate said. "I actually prefer the bar most of the time."

She led the way and they snatched two seats and got settled in. Kate ran her fingers across the white marble bar top. "This is absolutely gorgeous."

Zach agreed. "It's really a great slab. They did a great job making those rounded cuts."

Kate took in the atmosphere. It was a mixture of rustic elegance: comfortable, yet upscale. She picked up the menu to read the offerings.

"How about the ricotta meatballs and focaccia to start?" Zach asked.

"Mmm... that sounds delicious," Kate agreed, and then asked the waiter for the wine list.

They looked at the list together, and saw a few Texas wines, but mostly Italian.

"I suppose it would be okay to veer off the usual track and choose a chianti?" Kate asked Zach.

"That's fine with me." He ordered a bottle of Classico for them and turned slightly in his seat to face her.

Kate watched the bartender opening the bottle and Zach encouraged her to take the first sip before the bartender poured full glasses. She noticed the difference right away with the touch of tart cherries and lingering smokiness.

"Delicious." She nodded to the bartender to pour the rest. The restaurant was humming with conversation and jazz music playing lightly in the background.

"You know what surprised me?" Kate asked Zach, not waiting for his response, "How many new wineries have popped up on 290."

Zach shook his head as he swirled the wine in the glass. "Yes. I have been thinking the same thing. I'm not sure how many have opened since last year, but I think it's quite a few."

The bartender chimed in, "Thirty-five new wineries have applied for permits within the last six months."

"Whoa!" Kate exclaimed.

The bartender continued, "I have a friend on city council. It's unbelievable how the wine trail has grown in just three to five years."

"Are they mostly Texas wineries? Or, folks from out of state?" Kate asked.

"A healthy mix of both, I think," he said as he

cleaned the water stains off a wine glass with a white napkin. "But, you know, the biggest influx this past year has been from California."

Zach and Kate nodded in agreement before she spoke, "Seems sort of strange they would leave California to come out here. The terroir is so different."

"Cost, more than likely. And taxes," Zach said. "I think it's harder nowadays to run and manage a vineyard and winery in California because of all the regulations, and the taxes are astronomical. It's still cheaper to come out here."

"But how can the wine trail support all these wineries? Are there enough tourists to go around?" Kate asked as she took another sip of wine.

"There's over 65 wineries on the wine trail now," the bartender said. "But, amazingly, I think they're all doing well."

"The wine clubs really help, too" Zach added. "Folks find one or two wineries they really feel comfortable at, join them, and then they keep coming back every quarter for the pickup parties. It really helps stabilize the ebb and flow of tourist traffic throughout the season."

Their food arrived and just in time as Kate was getting really hungry. She cut into the large meatball and the cheese oozed out with a gorgeous waft of garlic. She put half on her smaller plate and then added a slice of the warm focaccia with an olive oil drizzle. They took bites, taking in the flavors, then washed it down more Chianti.

Zach wiped some tomato sauce off his mouth. "Dennis has been telling me that there's concern about available resources. It takes a lot of water to maintain a vineyard, especially in this dry region."

"The drought last year was real, and they say this year will be worse," the bartender said, as he topped off their glasses.

Kate shook her head, "It doesn't seem right

to stress the land so much. At some point something's got to give."

"Ready to order?" the bartender asked.

"Absolutely," Zach said, motioning for Kate to go first.

"I'll have the Linguine Nero," she said as he nodded.

"I'll do the Pappardelle," Zach said, and handed him the menu.

They enjoyed a moment of silence, taking in the lively ambiance. Kate pondered the implications of more wineries opening as she took another long sip.

"Tell me, what's happening with your book? Have you heard any news?" Zach asked.

Kate swallowed, letting the red wash down her throat before answering. "Not yet. Margaret said she got the final draft and said something about fast-tracking it, but I'm not sure what that means." Kate looked up at him over her glass. "She can be cryptic sometimes."

He nodded. "It's a New York thing, I'm sure."

Kate laughed. "Yeah, in all the years I've known her, you'd think I'd know what to expect, but she keeps surprising me. Keeps me on my toes."

Just then, their plates arrived, and they sat back to enjoy the presentation. The dark inky pasta stood in bold contrast to the shiny white china. Large pink gulf shrimp sat majestically on top, decorated lightly with fresh parmesan.

"That looks delicious," Kate said as she motioned to Zach's plate of gorgeous thick ribbons of pasta covered in a bolognese sauce with a dollop of ricotta in the center.

"Yours too. Bon appetit!" he said as he plunged his fork into the center of his pasta and began to swirl it around.

They ate in companionable silence, savoring the meal. Zach's phone buzzed on the bar top and he turned it over to check and then put it face down.

"Chloe. She got back home fine," he said between bites. "It makes me nervous having her driving back and forth between Austin every day, but she insists."

"It's not that far," Kate said. "I'm sure glad she was able to help out this summer."

"Yes, with Lillie and Paul in France, and the shortage of workers, I would have been in trouble," Zach said after wiping his mouth with a napkin.

"What do you mean shortage?" Kate asked.

"Well, it's really hard to find help here. Mostly because there aren't any rentals. There's a ton of Airbnb's and hotels, but not enough housing for locals. And what is available is overpriced."

"Gosh, I never really thought about that," Kate mused. "Lucky that Lillie and Paul were able to snag that room for rent on Dennis' property."

"Indeed," Zach said. "He's been offered a lot

more for rent you know, but he wouldn't think of it. He's a solid man."

Kate nodded in agreement. Dennis had a way about him. He was a big man of few words, but what he said was impactful. The fact that he insisted that Lillie and Paul stay on his property was just a testament to his generosity and how much he cared about them all.

They finished up their dinner and drained the last of the bottle. Zach paid the bill and then turned to Kate. "Any chance I can persuade you to stay at Chez Moi?" He gave her a seductive smile as he ran his fingertips lightly against her forearm.

Kate tingled in excitement. "Oh, I think I could be persuaded…" she trailed off and wove her fingers into his, making a braid.

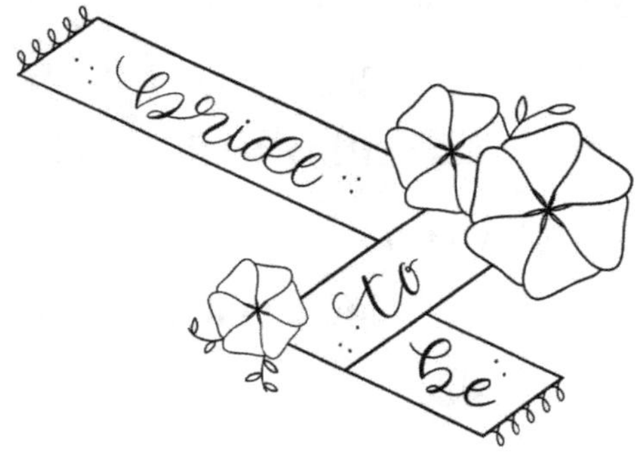

Eight

Chloe pulled into the parking lot and turned off her Prius. It was mid-morning, and she was meeting Chase for another pre-work coffee. It had become their sort of ritual. Every morning, she'd drive in and he'd be seated at their discreet table having already ordered their usual.

She stepped through the front door and waved to Melody behind the counter. "Morning,

Chloe!" the barista sang out, and motioned her head to Chase already in back.

Chloe nodded in acknowledgement and made her way to their table. Chase stood up, his height commanding, as he leaned down to give her a friendly hug. "Hey! How was your night?" he asked, getting settled back into the wrought iron chair.

"Too quick!" Chloe laughed as she set her purse on the table.

"Dude, that drive definitely cuts into your free time I bet."

"It does, but I don't mind," she said. "I actually love driving, and it gives me a chance to unwind."

"Speaking of business, how is your dad's tasting room going? We've been slammed lately."

Chloe nodded, tucking her blond hair behind her ears. "Same. I swear, we may have to hire additional help. It's been kind of nuts with all the bachelorette parties."

He chuckled. "Wait until you hear about the latest one we had. OMG. One hot mess."

Chloe laughed with him and enjoyed seeing his full smile and white teeth. She wondered if he could get any cuter.

Just then, Melody came over with their drinks—his caramel latte, and her cappuccino.

"Tell me!" Chloe exclaimed as she took a tentative sip off the top of the foam.

"Well, let's just say, it started off okay. Twelve ladies in pink sashes showing up after having been to two other tastings."

Chloe's eyes grew wide and Chase nodded.

"Yup. Probably should have taken that as a sign." He took a sip before continuing. "But one ended up trying to get on top of the bar to dance. Another was in the bathroom forever being sick."

Chloe palmed her forehead as he continued.

"But the kicker? The soon-to-be bride ended up getting in a fight with her beau over the phone and then drunk cried in the corner for an hour." He sat back, pleased with his retelling of the story.

"Oh. My. Gosh," Chloe said. "What the heck?"

They laughed together in understanding. It was like they were in a secret club, privy to the behind the scenes on the illustrious wine trail. Chloe loved being able to share stories with him.

"What's wrong with these people?" she asked, shaking her head. "It's like they come here and forget any sense of manners and normalcy."

"Yup. We're like a Texas wine cruise ship that never docks." He laughed at his own analogy before taking another sip.

"But seriously, it has been kind of crazy, right?" Chloe asked him as she checked her phone for the time.

"Yeah, but that's not the strangest thing." Chase raised his eyebrows at her and leaned forward.

Chloe was intrigued as he continued in a half-whisper. "Did you hear what happened at Slate Theory?"

Chloe shook her head, her eyes urging him to continue.

"Someone tampered with their barrels."

"What? Like, what do you mean, tampered?" Chloe asked, her head bent to see if anyone else was in earshot.

"Someone drilled small holes into some of the barrels. They went bad from air exposure."

"Oh my gosh," Chloe whispered. "But who would do that? How?"

Chase shrugged. "Dunno. There wasn't evidence of a break-in. Looks like it could be an inside job? But either way, that's thousands down the drain and some really expensive long-aged juice too."

"Wow." Chloe had another sip of her coffee and took it all in. Tampering at a winery? It seemed so strange. She had always thought of Fredericksburg as being a safe, welcoming, and trusting community. Was that changing? Or was it never true to begin with?

They finished their coffees and he walked her to the front. They both peered out the door to make sure no one saw them together.

"You go first," he said, but first gave her a big, warm hug.

Chloe hugged him back and then looked up at him. "See you tomorrow?"

"You bet." He grinned at her and added, "Be safe out there!"

"You too! Watch out for the pink sashes!" She laughed and then turned to walk out the door towards her car. As she got in and turned on the ignition, she thought about how this summer was getting stranger and stranger.

⇒ Nine ⇐

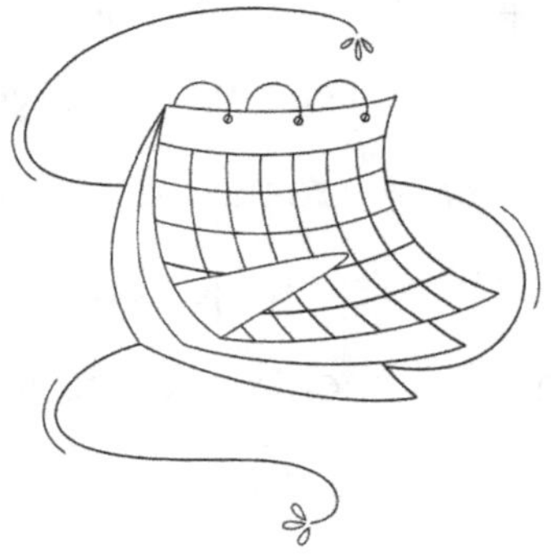

Kate had just pulled her Durango onto Hwy 290 after having another lovely breakfast with Zach at Sunset Grill. She was getting used to their routine. Even though he wanted her to stay over more, she thought they had found a nice balance with her visiting a few nights a week, then returning to her trailer in Spicewood. She relaxed back into her seat for the drive when her phone rang through the hands-free system and she saw Margaret's name pop up on the console.

"Hello!" Kate said brightly.

"Are you sitting down?" Margaret asked.

"Well, in a way. I'm driving."

"Good," she charged on. "I have some big news for you. *Big.* We're pushing up your launch date because there's a major chain that wants *your* book in all of their stores nationally!"

Kate swallowed hard. "What? That's amazing! Who?"

"Target. And that's not all. They're in the process of launching a new branding campaign with author events on site, and they want you as one of the first authors to kick it off."

Kate could hardly believe it. "Seriously? That sounds great, but what exactly does that mean?"

"It means we're busting our butts to get your book out in time so you can go on a national tour," Margaret said.

"National tour?" Kate asked as she held the steering wheel a bit tighter.

"Yes. My team has it all organized. We'll be sending you the calendar by the end of the day. You'll start in two months."

"Oh my gosh! That soon?" Kate buzzed with excitement.

Margaret was all business. "Now, normally we'd coordinate hotels and rental cars, but since you have your trailer, we can just give you a stipend to book RV spots if that's okay with you?"

"Um, yes!" Kate was thrilled. She could hardly believe the good fortune. "Once I have the dates I can start lining it all up."

"One more thing," Margaret said before she finished. "The tour is going to last a year."

"A year?" Kate was incredulous.

"Yes, I know that's a long time, but Target insisted on a full year commitment in order to launch the new branding properly. Is that going to be a problem?"

Kate replied without thinking, "Yes. No. I mean, that should be fine."

"Good. Then we'll send you the details and contract by email and I'll be in touch soon."

Margaret hung up and Kate sat stunned in her seat. A year-long book tour? Target stores nationwide?

She was beyond excited. Getting paid to travel all over the country in her Airstream? It was unreal. Then, as she watched the Hill Country scenery move past, a heaviness hit her. What about Zach? Away from him for a full year? She shuddered a bit wondering how he would take this news. And, what about Lillie? She had moved there from the Pacific Northwest to have the baby in the Hill Country and be closer to Kate. She hated the thought of disappointing her sister, or missing out on any moments with Emma. Just as her family was coming together, she was going to leave?

Kate decided to wait on telling Zach until she was sure. She instinctively dialed her best friend for advice.

Caroline answered on the first ring. "Well, Howdy-do! What's shakin', bacon?"

"You're never going to believe this," Kate said, and then launched into the whole story.

"Oh, my lawd! Gurl, you have some luck!" Caroline drawled in fascination. "I take that back. It's not luck because you deserve every bit of it."

Kate laughed. "Thanks, Car. But it's still pretty unbelievable. I'm just glad that my home is on wheels and I can take it with me!"

Caroline laughed with her. "Things happen for a reason."

"Only thing, I'm worried about telling Zach," Kate said.

"Really? Why?"

"He's been hinting more and more about me staying with him in town, and even though I like our one to two nights a week sleepovers, I know he wants more."

"Well, I suppose there's only one way to find out, sugar," Caroline tried to reassure her. "Just gotta rip that Band-Aid off and hope for the best."

"And what about Lillie..." she trailed off.

"Lillie is a grown woman with a wonderful support system, thanks to you. I'm sure she'll be right as rain."

Kate sighed deeply. "They always say when one thing goes well in your life, something else has to give."

"Speaking of..." Caroline trailed off with a dramatic pause. "You may have a visitor soon."

"What? Who?" Kate asked.

"Yours truly, of course," Caroline said, but her voice was no longer sing-song.

"What's going on, Car?"

"I'll explain when I get there. But I need to come visit for a week or so. Do you think you could help me find a place to stay? Maybe the adorable trailer that Lillie stayed in at your park?" Caroline asked hopefully.

"Of course! I'll see about it as soon as I get back. When are you coming?" Kate asked.

"Next week?" Caroline said, quickly adding, "I know it's short notice, but I could use some time with my dear friend."

"You're welcome anytime, Car. I hope you are okay?" Kate ventured.

"Oh, I will be. You'll see. Can't keep a Southern woman down for long," Caroline said. "I've got to run, but just let me know about the rental. I can give you my credit card if you need."

"No worries. I'll handle it and text you once I have it confirmed," Kate said.

They hung up and Kate didn't know what to feel. The excitement about her book tour took a backseat to her worry for her friend. She'd never known Caroline to be so muted. There was a heaviness in her voice that alarmed her and made her wonder what had happened.

———

It was after midnight, and Kate had been tossing and turning in bed, unable to get to sleep. The excitement of the book tour opportunity, and the dread of telling Zach and Lillie, kept her mind buzzing. She finally gave up and got out of bed to sit at her dinette. Her shades were drawn closed, and when she flicked the microwave light on, the warm glow made the space feel even more cozy.

She looked at her phone and decided to try to call Lillie. It would be early morning in France, but she knew her sister liked to wake up to the sunrise. She couldn't wait any longer and pressed the button on the phone, listening for a long moment before she heard the first ring.

"Sis?" Lillie's soft voice answered.

"I hope I didn't wake you?" Kate fingered the frayed edge of a placemat.

"No, I'm out on the patio having my quiet time before Emma wakes up. Are you ok?"

Kate took a deep breath. "Yes, but I have some news, and I just couldn't wait to share with you."

"Is it about your book?" Lillie asked.

"Yes. They want me to do a national book tour at Target stores!" Kate could hardly contain her excitement.

"Oh! That's fantastic! I'm so happy for you!" Lillie said.

"But, there's a catch," Kate continued. "That's why I'm calling."

"Okay..."

"It's a year-long tour that starts in a few months." Kate stated.

"A whole year? Wow... that's a long time." Lillie said.

"Yes, and I'm a bit conflicted about leaving you and Emma for that long," she finished.

"Sis, you don't need to worry about us. I have Paul, and we have our friends and community that we've built up in the Hill Country," Lillie's voice was tender. "I appreciate your concern, but you should definitely take this opportunity. Honestly, it's like you were preparing for it by living in an RV already."

Kate breathed out relief. "I'm so glad you understand. I didn't want you to think I was just abandoning you after you moved down here."

"I know that's not the case, and I also know that your talent shouldn't be confined to one place. This is an incredible opportunity for you to share your books with a wider audience, and I love this for you!" Lillie gushed. "Tell me more!"

Kate opened up her laptop to the email from Margaret, and filled her sister in on the itinerary, cities she'd visit, and the preliminary logistics. Then, she opened up the contract.

"So, I guess I'll sign the contract…" she trailed off.

"Do it. I'm so proud of you!" Lillie said before they hung up.

Kate felt relief and excitement as she read through the contract. She created her electronic signature and clicked through all the boxes until she reached the last one. With a quick prayer, she clicked *finish*.

Ten

Kate was busy at her dinette table inputting line items into a Google Sheet. She had received the preliminary set of dates for the book tour and it was a long list that spanned the whole country. It was overwhelming. She input the dates, city/state, then looked up RV parks nearby on Campendium and began booking spots. She also pulled up RV Life Trip Wizard so she could map out the routes between destinations. It was a massive undertaking, and she was only through a handful of dates when her phone rang: Zach.

She felt nervous butterflies in her stomach as she pressed the speakerphone. "Hey, Doc!" she said, trying to sound normal.

"Is this a bad time to talk?" Zach asked.

"Oh, no, I always have time for you." Kate shut her laptop so she could focus. "What's up?"

Zach cleared his throat and dove in, "Well, I have bad news. Remember how we were talking about the water shortage? Well, it seems like it's really hitting folks hard this year. Dennis just told me that one of his old friends who had a homestead for over 75 years has to move. His property was stuck between some of the newer vineyards and now his well is dry."

"Dry? Can't they dig deeper?" Kate asked.

"They tried. Still not enough water. The property around him is using too much with their irrigation systems."

"But that's crazy. Wouldn't the city do something about this?" Kate said.

"You'd think. But, sadly, there isn't much to be done. The land was sold, and with it the water rights. Maybe if they were on the city water and sewer, but even then it probably wouldn't make a difference." Zach exhaled heavily into the phone.

"Wow. I just can't believe it. That seems so unfair," Kate said.

"Yeah. Apparently it's due to all the new vineyards. The water table could withstand the old, grandfathered land, like Dennis' vineyard. But it's the new developments are taking a toll."

"What can be done?" Kate wondered out loud.

"Well, there's a city council meeting that we're going to attend. Not sure what good will come of it. I have a suspicion that the city is taking money and looking the other way."

"Geez, well, keep me posted. Your vines are doing okay, right?" Kate asked him as she sat back and peered out the window of her trailer watching the sun just starting to set.

"Yes, thankfully. We're lucky with our location." Zach cleared his throat again. "How are you doing?"

"Oh, fine. Just fine…" She trailed off deciding that it wasn't a good idea to share her news with him just yet. "I'm just getting some stuff done here and enjoying another beautiful Texas sunset."

"Great. Well, I won't keep you. I sure wish I were there watching with you though."

"Me too. I was just about to pour a glass of wine, and I'll have a little toast to you," she said sweetly, ignoring the warning in her gut.

They hung up, and she felt guilty for not being one hundred percent honest with him. After all, he might actually be really happy for her. Yet, she felt as though she were very close to the balloon popping, and her news might be the needle.

She got up to pour herself a glass of Tempranillo and stepped outside to sit in her patio chair and watch the sunset blanketing the sky with deep oranges and pinks against the darkening blue. A familiar star peeked out and Kate smiled as she took a nice long sip. She decided to keep her secret for just a little longer.

Eleven

Chloe was behind the bar wiping off the counter when her dad came in from the store-room carrying a case. "This should be enough to restock for tomorrow," he said as he set the case on top of the bar and began gently pulling the bottles out one by one.

"That party today wiped out our Viognier," Chloe said. "I think that's become a crowd favorite."

Zach nodded. "It's a really great release. Do you need help with those glasses?"

Chloe shook her head. "Nope. I'm nearly done."

Just then she saw a familiar red flash through the storefront window and looked out to see Chase and his father Peter peering in. She froze, not sure what to do, and that's when Zach saw them as well.

Peter waved through the window in his usual cocky way. Zach just barely nodded and turned away to walk back to the storeroom for another case. Peter turned to walk on, and Chase lingered behind him to give Chloe a tiny wave and guilty shrug before catching up with his father.

Chloe let out a low whistle and turned back to clean the final glasses. Her father came back in with another case. "I thought we had enough?" she asked,

He cleared his throat. "Won't hurt to add a few more."

Chloe paused and then decided to press him, "Hey, have you spoken to Peter since everything happened?"

"Nope." Zach stated without a hint of emotion as he pulled out the bottles.

"Huh. So, I guess you two are never going to make up?"

Zach looked up at her. "I don't think that's really a possibility. I have forgiven him and moved on, but he's not someone I'd like to be friends with again."

"I get it." Chloe felt discouraged, wondering how she was ever going to tell her father about Chase. They were becoming really good friends, and she hated keeping anything from him. She also knew from experience how her dad avoided conflict. He preferred to focus on things he could control, and once he made a decision about something, it was final. She wondered how she could ever get him to change his mind.

"Well, I'm going to take off unless you need anything?" she asked as she folded up a dish towel and placed it on the sink.

"That's fine, dear. Just text me when you get home." Zach came over to give her a bear hug and peck on the cheek.

"Always do." She grinned at him and then spun around on her heels to head out. Once outside, she looked down Main Street to see if she could catch another glimpse of Chase, but he was gone.

Twelve

Kate had picked up Caroline from the airport. Before heading to the RV park, she decided to stop off at Stone House Vineyard for a bite to eat and to catch up over a glass of wine.

"Oh, this is just gorgeous," Caroline said as they settled into a table on the patio overlooking the vineyard.

"Just wait, once we have our wine I'll take you over to the members area—it's a cliff overlooking Lake Travis. It's breathtaking," Kate said as they perused the paper tasting menu.

Choices made, they sat back and Kate looked at her friend, wondering how much longer she'd have to wait. "What's really going on, Car?"

Caroline took a deep breath, smoothing the wrinkles in her linen pants. "Well, it's really not that big of a deal. Rob and I have separated."

Kate gulped. "What? Car! How? Why?" She could hardly put together a sentence. The waiter came back with their glasses giving Caroline time to take a sip before continuing.

"It's actually been going on for a while." She fingered the long stem of the wine glass. "We've just drifted apart really. He's been sleeping in the guest house for the last few years."

Kate thought back and realized that she hadn't seen the two of them together since she visited before her own separation three years ago.

"Wow. Car, why didn't you tell me?" Kate asked.

"Oh, shoot. This happens to so many couples. And we didn't want to even breathe the word divorce until the kids were a bit older." Caroline took a long sip of the Mourvèdre, letting it slide down her throat.

"Are you going to divorce?" Kate nearly whispered.

Caroline shrugged. "Who knows? When we're together we fight about everything, so we just coordinate our calendars to keep appearances, but live separate lives in private."

Kate took a moment to let it sink in. Her mind thumbed back through the images of Caroline and Rob so happy every time she came to visit. It was hard for her to think that it could have been a façade. If a great relationship like theirs could hit the rocks, it made Kate question marriage or a deep commitment even more.

"I think that it's starting to hit harder

now that the kids are more grown," Caroline admitted. "I'm just not sure I'm ready to face the reality of divorce."

"Can't you go to couples therapy or something? Car, you've been together for over twenty years!"

"Don't I know it." She sighed deeply. "We'll see. That's why I needed to come out here for a break, to clear my head." Caroline raised her glass of wine. "To get some perspective."

Kate nodded, staying quiet for a moment.

"He says all I've ever cared about are the kids. That I don't put him first," Caroline continued. "I say all he's ever cared about is his damn job and golfing every weekend with his friends." She took another sip and then looked up at Kate. "Truth is? I'm not even sure we like each other anymore. There's just been so much water under the bridge that we've muddled along. But now, the thought of being together alone, without the kids, is honestly terrifying."

Kate began to see the whole picture. "I can understand that. There's a lot more pressure in the South to make it work, even when it doesn't," Kate said from experience, remembering how hard it was to divorce her ex-husband. It had been a horrible divorce, and she lost many friends after they chose his side. Of course, he made sure that his version of the story got out first—painting the picture of Kate as an immature woman who wasn't ready for love and left for no reason.

Kate still got angry thinking about his hidden infidelities, and the great lengths she took to be a devoted wife. In the end, she had to trust herself, even if it meant facing the brunt of public opinion.

"Southern traditions be damned!" Caroline finally started to get a spark back into her voice. "I've done my duty as the mother and wife. Now? I want to figure out what I want. It's high time I take care of myself."

Kate raised her glass to toast with her friend in agreement.

"Car, whatever you choose, you know I'm behind you one million percent, right?" Kate said as she gave her arm a squeeze.

"Oh, darlin'. Of course." Car patted the top of her hand. "You're the reason I'm even able to to think about a different life."

Kate raised an eyebrow. "Really?"

"Oh, yes. What you went through with David, it was inspiring. You trusted yourself and made a life that I never would have imagined." Caroline motioned her arm through the air around them for emphasis.

Kate smiled in realization. "Well, I didn't feel all that inspired at the time. It was out of survival." She thought back to the gaslighting, the lies, and emotional abuse. "I'm just grateful to be free of all that."

"Yes, but you did it. Yourself." Caroline nodded to her. "To have the guts to flip your life upside down. And you're happier than I've ever seen."

Kate blushed. "I am happy. And I wouldn't change one thing. But you can do this too, Car. You're one of the strongest women I know."

Caroline shook her head. "Naw, I have a lot of bravado, but underneath it all, I'm not sure I have the guts to back it up. I hate to admit it, but I care far too much what other people think."

"Come on. Let's take a walk," Kate said as she pulled her friend out of the chair and they walked arm in arm to the other side of the property.

A lovely breeze gently rustled the leaves on the live oak trees as they passed by. Getting closer to the edge, they could finally see the lake.

"Wow! I had no idea we were up so high," Caroline said as she ventured closer to the cliff's edge.

Kate nodded and thought about how these life-changing decisions were as dramatic as this tall cliff. Without knowing, you'd think the land went on forever, until you got up closer and saw the jagged edges. That rocky face descended sharply down a long distance before ending abruptly at the water's edge. She watched boats navigate the twisty currents below, seemingly oblivious to them peering down from above.

"That looks so refreshing," Caroline said as she sat down on a large, flat limestone slab to take in the view.

Kate sat beside her. "You have to get down that rough terrain to experience smooth sailing."

Caroline leaned into her friend. "Oh, you wise young thing." They took a last sip from their glasses as a turkey vulture swooped gracefully on the breeze, making long arcs between the cliffs.

Thirteen

The special session of the Fredericksburg City Council was called to order and everyone stood with their right hand over their hearts to say the Pledge of Allegiance. Once seated, the mayor began right away, "The purpose of this meeting is to open the door for a discussion and workshop on this issue of water usage as it pertains to the increased land development for agricultural purposes related to local wineries. No decision will be made by Council, but instead we will open the door to listen to you, and for you to listen to each other."

Chloe squirmed in her seat next to her father. The room was packed, and a few rows over she spied Chase next to his father Peter. Dennis was seated on the other side of Zach, the lines in his face etched deep.

The mayor continued, "We only have one microphone for comments, so please speak loudly so everyone can hear. We'll begin with a presentation from the director of Public Works and Utilities."

The presentation began and behind the podium, a large projection screen showed graphs. "As you know, the city of Fredericksburg relies solely on groundwater for its water supply. The primary source is the Ellenburger aquifer. You can see in these graphs that we have been monitoring the water levels at our two primary well fields over the past year. The Knauth well field has four groundwater wells, and the Old San Antonio Road well field has three. Compared to last year's usage, aside from the normal seasonal rise and fall, there is a drop in overall level," he stated.

Chloe eyed Dennis as his face twitched slightly.

"Now, this data isn't conclusive, we are sharing our findings as they pertain to this discussion."

The mayor opened up the floor for comments and Dennis rose immediately. "Now, you can't tell me that this isn't the result of overdevelopment. My family has been here for generations, and we've never experienced anything like this before."

Murmurs rose from the audience as another citizen agreed. "You all heard about Dwight Jackson's homestead? After generations, he has to move away because his well is completely dry."

Dennis continued, "How is the City going to

help those of us who have our own wells coming from the same aquifer? If the overall level keeps dropping, we're in for more than a drought."

A small commotion began in the audience and the mayor stepped in. "We hear your concerns, and that's why we are here, to try and discuss options."

"The only option is to stop letting outsiders come in and buy up our land to build more wineries," Dennis said, pointing a finger in Peter's direction.

Chloe's wide eyes matched Chase's as Peter stood up. "Don't point at us, Dennis. We don't even have a vineyard here."

"And that's an entirely different problem. You're shipping your California wine here and selling it with Texas labels," Dennis retorted.

"Gentlemen, let's keep this civil and on point," the mayor said.

Dennis and Peter sat down, but not before glaring at each other.

Chloe sunk down in her seat a bit and tried to get a glimpse of Chase out of the corner of her eye. All she could see was the flush of red in Peter's tanned cheeks.

Zach stood up. "We're all here for the same reason, to make sure we do our due diligence and protect our water supply. I think we can all agree on that, right?"

More murmurs in the gallery.

He continued, "At what point should we begin to be really concerned with the drop in levels? Can we halt or slow down the permits until we can be sure that the aquifer can support the growing number of wineries and vineyards?"

The director responded, "We are certainly monitoring this more closely now, as we are beginning to see a trend. We'll be happy to put together a report with our findings."

"Although we hear your frustration, we can't prevent people from buying land that is already zoned agricultural," the mayor chimed in. "But we could perhaps form a committee that will help monitor this better."

More citizens took the microphone to share their concerns as the secretary dutifully recorded the minutes. Chloe overheard Dennis whisper to Zach, "What we need to do is figure out a way to keep them out once and for all." A chill went down her spine.

Fourteen

After the meeting, Zach and Dennis approached Jack's Chophouse, a local favorite situated inside a 1930s American Foursquare house just off Main Street. They stepped through the front door and found a few seats at the already crowded bar. The atmosphere mixed elegance and comfort, with framed black and white photographs blanketing the forest green walls, checkered tablecloths, mounted elk heads, and crystal chandeliers overhead. Their seats were situated in front of the poster-size framed image of Marilyn Monroe biting her pinkie in thoughtful anticipation.

They waited their turn to order drinks and then began to debrief the council meeting.

"That was quite the meeting. At least the city is taking the matter seriously enough to warrant a special session," Zach said.

"Well, I don't see why we need to wait for a report to tell us what we already know," Dennis said. "It's clear that our resources are dwindling because of all the new wineries."

Zach cleared his throat. "Well, I think it's the rate at which those permits are being granted. But I agree, there should be more regulation."

"Forget regulation. We need to close the border," Dennis declared.

Zach chuckled slightly. "Well, Dennis, remember, we're from elsewhere too. Well, at least I am." He eyed his friend and partner.

"I wouldn't have been able to open my tasting room if that were the case."

Dennis shook his head. "Naw, we're using my grandfather's land for our vines. We were here way before anyone else, and we consider you part of the family."

They clinked their drinks and took a sip in agreeable silence.

"And, besides, all these new wineries are coming in from California. It's not just where they're coming from, but that they don't respect our customs or traditions here in Texas," Dennis continued.

"Meaning?"

"Meaning it's harder to grow and produce good wine here. It's tough farming. And we stick together to help each other out and share our resources on faith. It's the level of trust that we've built up over time." Dennis jerked his head up. "They just come in here and think they can do it all themselves. They exclude us, and not only that, they disrespect us thinking they can do it better without knowing a damn thing about this land."

Zach tried to smooth out the growing tension in Dennis' voice. "True. It's easy to think you know everything or can apply what's worked in one region to another. But I think there's an opportunity here for us to bridge that gap somehow and build more of a partnership, even if the partnership is just to protect the groundwater."

Dennis grunted slightly as he took another sip. "You can lead a horse to water, but you can't make him drink."

Zach smiled at the idiom and picked up his glass.

"I think the real opportunity is for us to form our own partnership among the Texas growers and wineries here in the Hill Country," Dennis said. "I'm not the only one fed up. I'm going to start reaching out to folks."

Zach grew uneasy as he began to realize his

idea of partnership and including everyone was probably exactly opposite of Dennis'. Once the fuse was lit, it was only a matter of time before the keg blew.

"Let's just see where we get at the next session. We'll get more data, and hopefully more support across the board." Zach finished his drink and motioned to the bartender for the bill.

Once outside, Zach saw the prominent G from the gold Freemason badge pinned onto Dennis' black leather vest. "I appreciate your help, Dennis, and I trust you," Zach said. "I just hope we can find common ground and get back to focusing on wine-making."

Dennis nodded. "You bet."

They parted and Zach couldn't help but wonder if what he said had fallen on deaf ears. He really didn't want to create more division in the community, just as he was becoming more accepted. He hoped that he could convince Dennis over time.

It was a beautifully sunny day in Spicewood and Kate decided to take Caroline to one of her favorite wineries in Stonewall. She rented her friend the same vintage 1955 Spartan trailer that Lillie had stayed in when she first arrived from France. Kate pulled her Durango up in front of the small deck that extended out from the side of the trailer, just as Caroline was securing the door.

She came down the steps, her brightly

colored kaftan flowing around her legs in the breeze.

"Helloo, my dear," she crooned as she leaned over to the driver's side to give Kate a peck on the cheek. Kate returned the gesture and then pulled out to head towards the winery.

"How'd you sleep?" she asked her friend as she turned right out of the RV park entrance.

"Like a babe," Caroline said. "It's been absolutely wonderful to be tucked away in that tiny trailer, like all my cares of the world were forgotten... even if just for a short while."

"Right? That's what I love about RV life. It's like you are on a permanent vacation."

"I have to admit that I never thought I would ever want to be away from my home in Pensacola. But this has me questioning things. It's wonderful to have a different perspective," Caroline said. "How about you? How is your book tour planning coming?"

"It's coming. But it's a lot of work, Car.

I've been at it for a week and only finished coordinating three months of the year-long tour so far. There's just so many logistics."

"That sounds like the worst part of it, right?" Caroline said. "After it's all mapped out, you can just enjoy being the amazing national book tour author that you are!"

They both giggled, and Kate drove on towards their destination. She loved having her friend close. The last time Caroline was there, it was all about Lillie and Paul's wedding, and there was just too much going on for her to really give her the attention she wanted. Thinking back, she wondered if she would have picked up on the separation sooner if she'd had more time.

A while later, after an enjoyable drive taking in the beauty of the Hill Country landscape, Kate turned left off Hwy 290 and pulled into the driveway for Adega Vinho Winery. As they drove slowly past the rows of vines, they could see clusters of grapes peeking out from underneath a canopy of large green leaves.

"Ooh! It must be getting close to harvest?" Caroline asked, as Kate pulled into a parking spot and turned off the ignition.

Kate nodded, turning to her. "I can't wait to experience my first harvest!"

"Fan-tastic!" Caroline squealed before they went inside the mid-century modern tasting room.

Once inside, they surveyed the bright room. It had a casual and open vibe with a watercolor motif and floor to ceiling windows overlooking the vines and live oaks beyond.

"Welcome!" the server said and suggested they find a spot where they felt comfortable.

The building was a trapezoid, which created uniquely designed spaces to lounge and taste. Kate motioned to the back of the room where there were two low couches across from each other with a coffee table between. They got settled in and the server came back with the tasting sheet for the day and two wine glasses.

"We'll start off your tasting today with the 2022 Branca Estate Reserve," he said and explained how the wine was oak barrel aged with malolactic acid, which made it more buttery than a usual vino verde. "And the Arinto is a Portuguese varietal that is extremely rare in Texas. We pride ourselves on planting and cultivating these varietals to bring a unique flavor to our wines."

He then poured the pale lemon-colored liquid into their glasses. "Enjoy! And please, relax and take your time."

As he walked away, they held their glasses up and toasted before bringing the glasses to their noses and taking a sniff and then tasting. The grapefruit, lemon, and slight apple taste was crisp and smooth on Kate's palate.

"This is so refreshing," Kate said.

"Makes me want to go to Portugal to

try it there," Caroline agreed and they took another sip.

"So, speaking of your book tour, have you signed the contract?" Caroline asked.

"Yes. It's official…" Kate trailed off.

"And what does Zach say about it?"

Kate made a guilty face and put her glass on the table. "I haven't told him."

"What? Kate, why on earth not?" Caroline exclaimed.

"Well, the last few times I've talked to him there's been all this bad news happening, and I just didn't want to add to it. I still have time…" Kate trailed off.

Caroline shook her head. "You're just being chicken."

Kate laughed. "Am not!"

Caroline's eyes were wide and accusing. "B'kaawk!"

They laughed, and then Kate got more serious. "I just really don't know how he'll take it. Every time we've been together since the wedding, he keeps pushing me to move in." She looked at her friend. "Remember when he wanted to buy a house for both of us?"

Caroline nodded, swallowing. "Yes. And if I remember correctly, he came up with a fine compromise of buying a house with an RV pad that you could hook up to."

Kate grimaced again. "Yeah, look how well that turned out."

"Well, I have wondered why that didn't work. What's holding you back, gurl?" Caroline's Southern drawl came out full-force now that she was a few sips into her wine.

"Honestly, I don't know." Kate looked up at her over her glass. Deep inside, she did know. She just wasn't ready to put a voice to it.

The server came back and asked how their first wine was before diving into the next one. "For our next tasting, we have the 2022 Estate Rosé. It's really our winemaker's passion. He's a six foot, five inch tall man who loves his pink wine." They all laughed. "This is made one hundred percent from our Mourvèdre and Tempranillo estate grapes that you can see right out these windows." He pointed to the view and they took it all in.

They watched as the rose-colored liquid filled their glasses, and then swirled it a bit before taking it on the nose.

"Mmm... I taste some strawberry notes," Caroline said.

Kate threw her head back and laughed, "You're starting to sound like a sommelier!"

"Well, just get me a few more tastings under my belt and I'll be a pro!" She winked at her friend and took another sip.

"Where were we? Ah, yes. You and your issue with living with men," Caroline poked at her friend.

Kate rolled her eyes. "I think this wine is bringing out your sass."

"Or the truth."

Kate took another taste and thought about it. "I think it was just too soon, Car. I had just finally gotten my feet back under me after the divorce, and I had finally written a best-seller." She looked at her friend. "Of course, meeting Zach was a once-in-a-lifetime kind of thing. And I couldn't believe that we'd found each other again. For that, I am so grateful." She swirled the rosé in her glass. "But, I'd just gotten used to being single again."

Caroline nodded, "Of course. Picture-perfect love story aside, it is a big step to move in with someone again. Especially after a nasty divorce."

"Really, I love my life in my little Airstream," Kate continued. "But, now I feel more and more that he's not happy with us living apart. How do you think he'll take hearing that I'll be gone for a whole year?"

"Darlin', hasn't he always been the most supportive of you? Why would he change now?"

Kate shrugged. "You're probably right. Maybe I'm just reading too much into things." She wasn't entirely convinced.

The server came back for their third tasting. "Now we have our 2020 Estate Pordosol. This is our first Estate version of our signature blend of forty percent Tempranillo and sixty percent Mourvèdre. Pordosol means sunset, and I think you'll agree that this is a lovely wine to sip while watching a gorgeous Hill Country sunset." He poured the red into their glasses.

Kate sat back and took the first sip, tasting a smooth blend with black cherry highlights and hints of spice.

"Oh, lawd... I think we may have to get a bottle of this to drink tonight on the deck." Caroline motioned her glass to Kate.

"Let's do it," Kate agreed.

"So, aside from the hesitation with Doctor Wine, how do you feel about the tour overall?" Caroline asked.

Kate hardly finished swallowing before she exclaimed, "Car, I'm so excited! As I start plugging these dates and cities into my spreadsheet, I can't help but think of all the people who will be buying my book!" She giggled in delight. "And I love meeting my readers in person. It's one thing to write a book and have it do well, but you're disconnected from the feedback, except reviews, if anyone bothers to write one." She took a quick breath. "But to meet them in person, it's really heart-warming to hear how my books have touched their lives."

Caroline leaned back into the couch. "You do make a difference, darlin'. It's more than your books, it's who you are. You're the whole package!"

Kate blushed. "If someone took the time to read my books, it's important to me that I take the time to connect with them in a more meaningful way."

"The tour sounds fabulous and meant to be! Maybe I can meet up with you for some of the dates?" Caroline suggested.

"I'd love that!" Kate reached for her glass out and they toasted in celebration, before draining the last drops.

Looking out the large windows, Kate thought about how very grateful she was. Maybe it was the wine, or her friend, or the view, but she felt joy tingling throughout her body.

The server returned for the final pour. "This is the 2020 Estate Touriga. It's also a varietal from Portugal and rare here in Texas. It tastes more like a petit syrah, on the jammy side and slightly sweeter."

Kate and Caroline enjoyed this last tasting in silence as they relaxed into the couch and took in the scenery and the hushed conversations going on around them. Kate let the floral blackberry taste delight her tongue and wash down easily as she basked in the company and the ambiance. She made the decision that she would tell Zach in the morning. It was time.

⇉ Sixteen ⇇

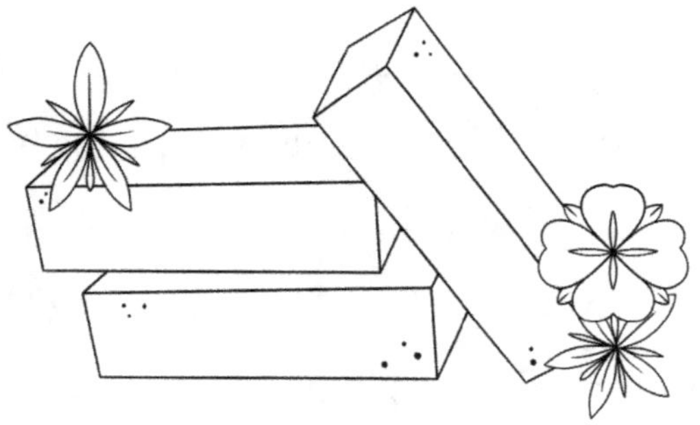

Main street was vacant, darkness inhabiting the spaces where hundreds of tourists had congregated earlier. The normally congested blocks now opened to a wide, long lane, flanked on both sides by dormant storefront windows. Yellow pools of light spilled onto the limestone bricks and out into the street, accentuating the shadows. The traffic lights ticked as they switched from red to green, oblivious to the absence of traffic.

A whippoorwill called out while a lazy armadillo poked around the buildings looking for a midnight snack. A sudden breeze rustled up some dead oak leaves making a scraping noise against the uneven sidewalks. A shadow moved between the buildings, swift and nearly imperceptible. Off in the distance, a dog barked a single call of warning.

A crash broke the silence as a brick flew through the All Points Between storefront, shattering the large picture window into tiny shards of glass that blanketed the sidewalk, the sharp edges refracting light. Stillness took over again, as the traffic light ticked to red.

ZACH WAS BY HIMSELF IN the tasting room enjoying the mid-morning rays of sunshine beginning to filter through the windows. He liked this time of the day, when he could gather his thoughts and do a last minute inventory check before Chloe arrived to help him open.

As he counted bottles, he thought about the last conversation he'd had with Dennis. The way Dennis had talked about keeping the outsiders out for good made him a little nervous. As much as Zach appreciated being considered an insider, with Dennis being his business partner and longtime friend, he knew that he wasn't really from here either. There was something that bothered him about excluding anyone. He understood Dennis' concerns about the land, resources, and culture, but he couldn't fully accept the idea of closing the Hill Country off to further growth. There had to be a way to co-exist—to work together in support of the history and legacy of this land.

A tap on the front door pulled him out of his thoughts. Looking up, he saw Kate waving through the window.

"Hi, this is a surprise," he said as he opened the door for her.

Kate leaned in to give him a quick hug, "I hope you don't mind? I just wanted to talk with you in person."

"Sure, of course," he said as he closed and locked the door behind her.

She turned around quickly to face him, "I have some news."

"Oh, great! Is it about your book?" he asked as he pulled out a barstool for her.

"Yes. Margaret called me, and my book has been chosen for nationwide placement... at Target," she said.

"That's amazing! Congratulations. I know you had a good feeling about this one," he said as he pulled her into a warm hug.

"There's more," she said as she pulled away from him. "There's also a book tour."

"Of course! That's great news, isn't it?" he asked, wondering why she seemed hesitant.

"It's a year-long tour," Kate blurted out.

"What? A whole year?"

"Um, yeah, they want this campaign to do well, so they are making it comprehensive. I'll be the first author to do book signings nationwide."

"Huh. So how would that work exactly? Would you be flying back and forth?" He leaned back into a barstool for support.

"Um, no. I'll be taking my Airstream," she explained. "Staying at RV parks along the way."

"For a year?" Zach was still trying to understand. He had been hoping that they could stay together more than just one or two nights a week, but the idea of her being gone for a year seemed unbelievable.

"It's a tremendous opportunity, and one I can't pass up," she said, as she reached out to tug on the opening of his button-down shirt.

"When would you leave?" he asked.

"In six weeks..."

"But Kate. What about us?" Zach pulled back and watched her fingertips fall.

"I still love you. I just need to do this for my career," Kate said softly, as she tried to pull closer to him.

Zach pushed her back and stood up. "Kate, I've been extremely patient with you."

"You have!" she quickly agreed, hoping to avoid having him elaborate.

"First, you're not wanting to move in, and then not wanting to even stay more than one or two nights a week. But this would mean a whole year apart from you. I don't think I can do that."

Kate's face clouded over. "I, uh, I just thought that it wouldn't be a big deal..." she trailed off.

"It is to me," he said.

"But, we could talk over the phone every night? Maybe you could fly out to meet me for some of the bigger cities?" Kate was now full-on pleading.

"No, Kate, I'm really happy for you, but you

have to understand, I've been divorced and single for a long time. I'm ready to be fully with someone. And I thought that someone was you." His voice was taut with emotion.

Kate's eyes welled up with tears. "So, what does this mean then?"

"I don't know." He turned away from her to walk to the other end of the bar.

He was beginning to feel the pressure of things piling up. First, the issues with Dennis and the other wineries, and now Kate wanting to leave him for a year. He needed some space to sort everything out.

"Chloe will be here any minute. Let's talk about this later," he said, turning to face her from across the room. His heart hurt watching her turn away to walk out the door.

⇾ Seventeen ⇽

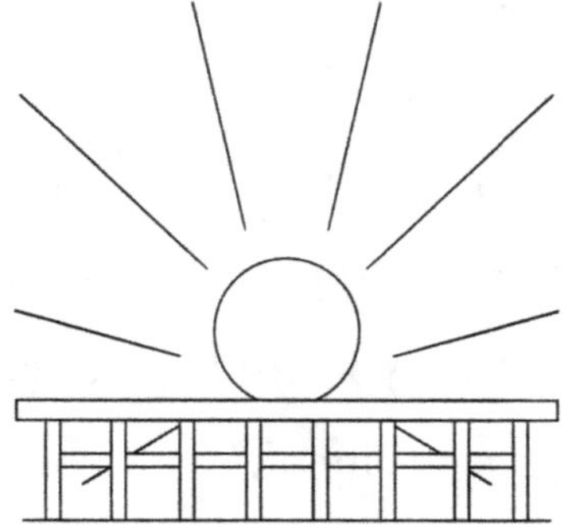

That evening, Kate sat out on Caroline's deck with a bottle of the Adega Vinho Pordosol, waiting for their own sunset.

"Gurl... I just can't believe he said that." Caroline sipped on her glass as they both sat overlooking the farmland beyond.

"Well, he did. And I guess I was the fool thinking that it would be different." Kate sipped and pondered. "Is it always going to be like this with men? That we either have to choose them or choose ourselves? Why can't we get both?"

"That's the age-old dilemma, darlin'," Caroline said. "You know men just aren't good alone. That's why so many older men remarry quickly, while most older women stay solo."

Kate thought for a moment. "I suppose that's true, but I really thought that if you find the right person, that you could balance independence with commitment."

Caroline shrugged. "I think sometimes you can. But it's less common than you think."

"So, what am I supposed to do? Cancel this tour?"

"Aw, hell no!" Caroline shook her head vigorously. "This is your life, and you should be damn proud of what you've accomplished. I'm afraid that he's going to have to understand. It's just a year."

Kate grimaced wondering whether that year would seem long or short. "It's just frustrating that I even have to question it at all. If the roles were reversed, I'd figure out a way to make it work. I'd never give an ultimatum." Kate's sadness was turning into indignation. "Why should I always have to sacrifice in a relationship?"

Caroline sipped her wine and was quiet for a moment. "I still have faith in our Dr. Wine. Maybe he was just in shock and needed some time to work it out in his mind. He does love you, and I doubt he wants to lose you again."

Kate took a deep breath hoping that her friend was right. "I guess we'll find out... if he ever calls again."

As if on cue, Kate's phone lit up and buzzed: Zach.

Caroline saw and excused herself to give her friend some privacy.

"Hey," Kate answered.

"Hi," he said. "Kate, look, I'm sorry about our conversation earlier. I was just taken by surprise. I really am sorry, and I want us to figure something out."

She breathed out in reply, "Me too! I don't want to lose you, Zach."

"You won't. At least, I don't think you will," he said. "I'm not sure that I can do a year of a long-distance relationship."

"I know it's not ideal."

"If you decide to go, let's just keep talking and see what we can figure out."

"I am going, Zach. I've signed the contract," she said.

He breathed out deeply and then said, "Well, then. We'll just have to get creative, won't we?"

"I guess so." She felt like it was progress, even if she wasn't sure which direction it would take.

"Look, Dennis is calling and I've got to take it. Can we talk tomorrow?"

"Caroline and I are coming by the tasting room in the afternoon," she said.

"Good. Okay, I'll see you then." He sounded relieved as he hung up.

Kate stared at her phone for a moment and then motioned for her friend through the window.

"Well?" Caroline stepped back out onto the patio.

"He apologized," Kate said.

"Good! See, I thought it would work out." Caroline poured herself more wine.

"Well, sort of. He still isn't sure about the year apart, but wants to talk tomorrow when we go visit." Kate took a big sip of her red, letting it wash down the bitterness.

"Okay, then. It's something. Give the man some time and I'm sure he'll come around to the idea," Caroline said.

"Yeah, I sure hope so." Kate looked out on the horizon as the sun was beginning to set. They sat quietly watching the oranges, pinks, and blues wash the sky as the day's light faded.

⇒ Eighteen ⇐

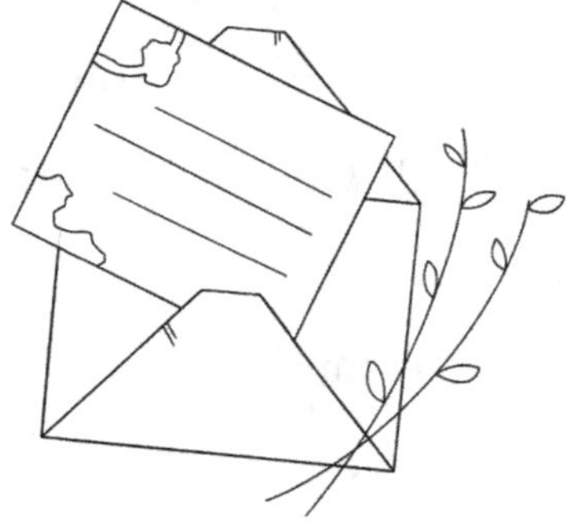

Chloe hurried into the cafe for her and Chase's usual morning rendezvous. She was running a bit late and waved at Melody as she quickly made her way to the back table.

"I'm sorry I'm so late!" Chloe was breathless as she gave him a quick hug. She pulled back and noticed that he wasn't as chipper as usual. Was he mad because she was late? "Are you okay?"

Chase shrugged before sitting down. "Dude,

you won't believe this." He motioned for her to sit down and then pulled a piece of paper from his back pocket.

Chloe watched as he unfolded it and then handed the white paper to her. It was a letter, dated the day before, from a group she hadn't heard of, the "Hill Country Wine Grower's Association."

She read it out loud. "It has come to our attention that the new vineyards that have come in over the last two years are creating a water shortage and threatening the livelihood of the original vineyards in the Hill Country. Furthermore, tasting rooms have popped up downtown that do not support Texas wine, but instead offer wine from California and elsewhere, which further removes support for our growers and vineyards."

Chloe's eyes were wide as she looked up over the sheet of paper at Chase.

He just nodded with his mouth set in a

line. "Yup. I think they are trying to pass something to bring to the city council to force us to close up."

"What? That's crazy! This is getting out of control." Chloe put the page down as Melody delivered her coffee.

"It's real," Chase said. "I knew that coming here was going to be way different from back home, but like this is some vigilante stuff."

Chloe shook her head. "Yeah, folks down here advertise that they carry guns and aren't afraid to shoot first and ask questions later. But, it's not like you're hurting anyone. It's just wine."

"I guess that's not what some of the old-timers think." Chase sipped his latté.

"I wonder if I should say something to my dad?" Chloe half-wondered out loud.

"Maybe? I feel like we're being targeted and, like, it sucks. My dad's worked hard, and spent a lot of money opening his tasting room. He's not going to shut down without a fight."

Chloe sat quietly thinking about how she would tell her father she even knew about the letter because he didn't know about her friendship with Chase. She really liked him and increasingly looked forward to their meetings.

"Ugh. I just don't know what to do. Maybe I'll poke around today and see if I can get some info," she said as she took another sip.

"I've also heard that we're being pegged for the weird stuff going on around town. Like, the tampering with the barrels at Slate Theory," he continued.

"Wait, how would you be involved with that?"

"Who knows?" he said exasperated. "I just think people are trying to come up with any reason to push us out."

"You don't think your dad could be doing anything behind the scenes, do you?" Chloe asked before realizing she may have overstepped.

"Absolutely not," Chase said firmly. "My dad's all about money, and hyper-competitive, but he's not a crook." He looked her squarely in the eyes and she believed him.

"I'm sorry, I shouldn't have asked that," she said.

"Don't be. I get it. Tempers are high, and rumors are flying. It's like riding a radical barrel wave, just gripping the rails and hoping you can use the force to propel yourself forward before it collapses and pulls you under." He grinned at her. "It's all about patience, skill, and timing."

She smiled thinking of how hot he would look on a surfboard, bare-chested and hair wet from the spray. She let that fantasy linger for a moment before realizing that he was staring at her.

"Oh, sorry." She giggled, blushing and pulling herself together.

He grinned, his green eyes sparkling, then looked at his watch. "We'd better get going."

"Yup. I'll let you know if I hear anything today," she said before grabbing her purse.

"Cool. I appreciate it." He smiled full this time and gave her a hug before they left the café separately to head to work.

Nineteen

Kate and Caroline arrived at the Winsome Winery tasting room dusty and thirsty, having just spent an enjoyable day meandering the grounds at Fredericksburg Trade Days. The monthly event was like a huge flea market spanning multiple barns with indoor and outdoor vendors, food, music, and even livestock. Caroline had made a point to take selfies with the black and white Oreo cows behind her.

Inside, the room was busy. Chloe was

attending to a large table of young women, with Zach holding court behind the bar. The cool air was welcome after being outside in the dry heat, and Caroline and Kate found two seats at the end of the long bar.

"Be right with you," Zach mouthed as he finished pouring a tasting of a red for a couple at the other end of the bar.

Kate felt awkward coming back to the tasting room after their meeting the other day. She wasn't sure where they stood now. Her mind buzzed with the thought of hitting the road in a few months, and she hoped that they would be able to navigate a long-distance relationship.

"Wowee, it's busier than a one-legged cat in a sandbox!" Caroline exclaimed as she surveyed the crowd.

Kate laughed in agreement as Zach approached. "Hello ladies! How are we doing today?"

"Hot and thirsty as all heck," Caroline said. "Is there a doctor in the house?"

They all laughed. "I've got just the cure for you," he said and then put his hand on the bar in front of Kate. "And for you." He winked at her and then turned around to fetch a bottle and two glasses for them.

Kate felt warmth in her cheeks from the gesture and thought maybe they would be alright after all. She turned to watch Chloe expertly deliver a tasting and then clear off a table within seconds.

"Hi, Kate!" she said, wiping an errant strand of hair away from her forehead with the back of her hand. "Hi, Caroline!" She came up behind the bar to deliver the dirty glasses to the sink and then came around to give them both half hugs.

"It's busy today," Kate said, stating the obvious as they pulled away.

"It really has picked up. Can't wait for Lillie

and Paul to come back so I have some extra help." She grinned and then turned to Caroline. "How has your trip been?"

"So good, I may never leave," Caroline said, smiling at Kate.

Zach poured them two large glasses of rosé, "This should get you started." Then he turned to attend to the other guests.

Chloe went back to her tables, and Kate and Caroline turned towards each other with a toast before taking a nice long sip of the refreshing and fruit-forward rosé.

The front door opened and Kate made out Dennis' figure and waved. He came right up to them, taking his cowboy hat off to give Kate a hug and then greeting Caroline. "Wonderful to see you again," he said as he held his hat against his chest and politely shook her hand.

"Oh, now, we're family, Dennis!" Caroline laughed as she pulled him in for a hug.

"How are things in the vineyard?" Kate

asked as she turned her barstool to face him. Even from the barstool, she still had to look up as he was considerably taller.

"Fine for the most part," he said, setting his hat back on his head. "The grapes are coming along nicely. I'm headed to Lubbuck early tomorrow to check on our blocks up there."

Caroline squealed, "Ooh, I sure wish I could be here for harvest!"

Kate nodded in agreement as Dennis responded, tipping his hat, "We'd love to have you, anytime m'am."

"Tell me, have things died down any?" Kate asked. "With the rumors around town and all."

Dennis' face grew tense. "Well, now I don't know about rumors, but I do know that we have a serious issue on our hands with all these outsiders coming in, and we're hoping to do something about it. We're forming a committee to help, how should I say, persuade these folks to reconsider making the Hill Country their home." He then politely excused himself as he made his way to Zach at the other end of the bar, leaving Kate wondering what exactly he meant by *persuade.*

"Ooh, wine drama!" Caroline chimed in as she took a healthy sip.

"It's pretty serious, with a water shortage affecting the livelihoods of the older vineyards and homesteads," Kate said. "Apparently, there's also been some mischief on the wine trail, so folks are taking sides."

"Who needs reality tv when you can experience the drama yourself with a nice glass of Texas wine?" Caroline raised hers in the air as Kate shook her head.

As evening drew near, Dennis said goodbye to Caroline and Kate before heading out. There were only a few couples lingering as they neared closing time. Zach was busy restocking while Chloe helped wash and dry the wine glasses.

"Dad, I was thinking that I might stay over a few nights?" Chloe said as she inspected a glass for water marks.

"I'd love that, honey. I'm sorry that we haven't had much time together except for working," he said, putting the box he'd just emptied on the floor.

"Oh, it's been great. But it has been busy, and with me driving back and forth I haven't had any time to get any photography done," Chloe said.

"I wish I could have given you more time away from the tasting room, but you've been essential." He gave her a sideways hug. "I couldn't have done it without you."

She grinned and gave him a quick peck on the cheek before getting back to the glasses.

"Zach, can we talk outside?" Kate asked.

"Sure," he said as he placed a white towel on the bar top and followed her to the patio.

As soon as she turned around, he took her hands in his and kissed them. "Kate, I'm sorry it's been so busy all day I haven't been able to break away."

She shook her head. "Oh, no. That's totally fine. It's your business."

He pulled her closer and she felt his warmth press against her as he lifted her chin and gave her a soft, long kiss. Her knees went wobbly as she leaned into him, never wanting it to end.

They separated just enough that Kate could still feel his breath against her lips.

"So, are we going to be okay?" she half-whispered to him.

He paused, before looking into her eyes. "Honestly, I'm not sure."

She swallowed hard, wondering what to say before he continued.

"Let's just see what happens. I need some time to process this, and we've got some time, right?" he said and kissed her firmly one more time.

"Yes, of course," Kate said after pulling

back, but she knew that time was ticking down quickly. What she really wanted was the reassurance that she wasn't going to lose him when she left.

She followed him back inside and met Caroline at the front. Zach approached her friend.

"You have a safe trip back to Pensacola."

Caroline gave him a big hug. "And you keep doing a fabulous job here in wine country, Doc."

Kate said goodbye to Chloe before heading out with Caroline. As the door closed and she faced Main Street, Kate could still feel the imprint of his strong lips against hers.

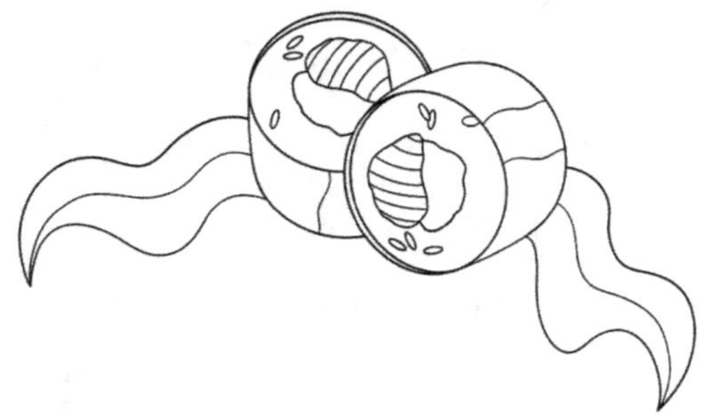

Twenty

The next day, Chloe was at the local H-E-B grocery store picking up a few items for her lunch when she felt her phone buzz in the pocket of her jeans.

She answered immediately, "Hey, Chase." Most of the guys her age loved to text, but she liked the fact that Chase preferred talking over the phone or in person.

"How's your day? Whatcha doin?" he asked in an easy manner.

Chloe was eyeing the sushi rolls in the large prepared food section. "Just trying to decide on whether to get a Dragon roll or California."

"Dude, get both. Hey, you wanna meet up for lunch?" he asked.

Chloe thought for a second. "How about you meet me here at H-E-B? We can grab a seat outside at the picnic table."

"Sweet. Grab me whatever you get, and I'll be there in ten minutes." He hung up. She loved how easy he was with everything. No drama, just good vibes. Chloe picked up a combo roll, and then grabbed them two waters before heading to the checkout.

It was bright and already warm outside when she made her way to the red table. She saw his tall lanky frame and waved. He smiled big, his hair was even brighter in the sun.

She stood up, and he gave her a big solid hug before pulling away. Chloe tingled a bit and looked around her to see if anyone was watching. Part of her wanted the world to see this cute guy hanging out with her. But the other part was wary of them being caught, so she slid down into her seat and tried to be inconspicuous.

"This is awesome. What do I owe you?" He made a move for his pants pocket while Chloe shook her head grinning.

"Nothing. It's on me today."

They poured soy sauce over their rolls and dug in, savoring the first few bites of salty fresh goodness.

"Anything new?" Chloe asked after swallowing a big bite.

Chase nodded. "My dad said he heard someone tampered with the equipment at the production facility."

Chloe's eyes grew wide. "What?"

"Yeah, they were running the machine to put the labels on their bottles and it stopped working." Chase raised his eyebrows. "I don't know how any of this works, but like, dude, they have to wait until it's fixed before they can get those bottles ready to sell."

Chloe was thoughtful for a moment. "So, you mean the bottles of wine your dad imported from outside of Texas?"

Chase nodded, "Yeah, he ships them here and then runs them through the machine to put our tasting room labels on."

Chloe wondered if it was a coincidence, or possibly something more. She took another bite as Chase continued. "Can you believe it's almost the end of summer and I haven't even gotten to see any of the vineyards for real," he said, running his hand through his thick hair.

Chloe had an idea. "Hey! Dennis is in Lubbock right now, so we could totally go to his vineyard and I can show you around." She realized with Dennis being away, her secret would still be safe. "Besides, I'm staying over with my dad so I can get more photography done. I'd love to get some great sunset shots of the merlot grapes before harvest."

"That would be awesome!" Chase perked up.

"How about we meet back here an hour before sunset, like 7:30? I'll drive us out there." She grinned as she finished up her lunch and started to gather up her trash.

He helped her put the rest in the trashcan and gave her a quick hug before heading to his car. "See ya later!"

She put on her sunglasses and waved as she made her way to hers. Chloe was excited about getting some great shots of the vineyard, and get to spend more time with Chase. It was almost perfect.

Twenty-One

Kate and Caroline were driving east on 290, away from Fredericksburg, when Kate had an idea. "Hey! We should stop by The Speakeasy before we head back. It has the coolest atmosphere, and fresh-made signature cocktails."

"I'm game!" Caroline said as she watched wineries and billboards go past her window.

Just past Messina Hof Winery, Kate pointed to the right and turned off 290. They pulled through a gated entrance with no signage and found a parking spot in front of what looked like a typical white Victorian house. The entire front of the house was a covered porch with two stair entrances.

Kate led the way, pointing to the comfortable lounge furniture on the patio. "After we get our drinks, we can sit out here. But, wait until you see the inside." She grinned as she opened the front door and they stepped inside.

The interior lived up to the establishment's name; the brightness of the exterior was completely replaced by dark gray walls, leather chairs, brass tables, and strategically placed lighting. It was indeed like stepping into another world that might involve a secret handshake or discreet nod.

"Ooh, this is absolutely fabulous!" Caroline exclaimed as she made her way around to take in the unique decor touches.

Kate pointed to the bar. "They have a special

cocktail menu. They use fruit from the farm out back and their own homemade spirits."

They made their way up to the bar. Rows of bottles of Salvation Spirits lined shelves on the back wall, and on the bar top stood clear mason jars of various sizes containing fresh and dried fruits, spices, and garnish.

The bartender handed them black pieces of paper with gold lettering that listed all the cocktails. He was wearing an apron with pockets containing different tools over a button-down long-sleeved shirt. His long blond hair was pulled back into a low ponytail.

"I'll try the espresso martini," Caroline said, after perusing the menu. "Make sure I get all three of those coffee beans, I need all the health, wealth, and happiness I can get!"

"Something with a little coffee would probably do me good," Kate said, and ordered the same.

They found a spot at a brass table with comfortable dark blue velvet chairs. "It takes a bit longer for the cocktails to be prepared, but it's totally worth it," Kate said as she got settled.

"I love how every place on the wine trail is different," Caroline said. "And having a break from wine is a nice change."

"Yeah, there really are as many choices as tastes here. From high-brow to low-brow, wine, beer, distilleries—something for everyone." Kate regarded her friend. "Are you ready to head back home?"

Caroline let out a long exhale. "Guess I better be. I can't keep away forever, time to face the music."

Kate nodded as the bartender came over carefully balancing their drinks so as to not spill a drop.

"This looks delicious," Caroline said as she took one of the tall glasses from him and took a sip. "Exquisite!"

Kate nodded in agreement as the bold

espresso delighted her palate and she tasted the Aztec chocolate bitters. "A perfect finish to a wonderful trip."

"I can't thank you enough for having me on such short notice," Caroline said.

"That's the great thing about RV life, it's not a problem at all. I still had my space and time to do what I needed," Kate explained.

"And I had time to do some good old-fashioned mulling," Caroline agreed.

"Did you figure anything out?"

"Naw, only that I will miss having you in such close proximity." They felt warmed by the cocktails and their friendship.

"Tell me, how do you feel about Dr. Wine and this book tour? He seemed to be alright today, so does that mean he'll be willing to give long distance a try?"

"Well, his kiss said yes." Kate fingered the stem of her glass. "But he said he still needed to process it."

"Oh, good grief. It's not like you'll be gone forever! And it's not like you're off running around—you'll be working!" Caroline waved her hand emphasizing the point.

"Truth is? I don't think we're on the same page in this relationship after all." Kate looked up grimacing slightly. "I'm starting to think that he wants us to move down the marriage track, and I'm not even sure I want to show up at the station."

"Do you mean you don't want to be with him at all?" Caroline prodded.

"It's not that," Kate said. "It's just that I like our relationship being committed but a little less defined. I like the freedom I have, and I think it makes our time together even more exciting."

Caroline made a noise. "Well, exciting doesn't always last. Trust me, I know."

Kate sat quiet for a moment. "I think that if I were to be honest, I'd never get married again.

Or even live with someone again." She watched for her friend's reaction.

"Well, now we're getting somewhere." Caroline leaned back. "You have to be honest with yourself about what you want and need. Because the only person who can make you happy is you."

Kate agreed, unfortunately She thought her whole life that what she wanted was the white picket fence, the ring on her finger, maybe kids, definitely a dog. Now, as she looked back in hindsight at her failed marriage, she realized that none of it really made her happy. That she was happiest living her dreams and working towards her own goals.

"Does that make me selfish?" Kate asked.

Caroline flicked her hand in the air as though she were parting smoke. "Not one whit. You see, not everyone is cut from the same cloth. And our experiences truly do shape who we are and will become. Somebody else's dream family might be your personal hell." She laughed. "You have to trust in here." She motioned to her belly and then to her heart. "And here."

Kate loved the way her friend knew exactly what to say, that she wasn't telling her what to do, but just helping her affirm what she already felt. Kate had a strong sense of her inner truth, of what she really needed to be happy. Especially after her marriage. She knew she had to trust herself.

"What about you? What does your gut say about your situation?" Kate turned the table.

Caroline pursed her lips. "My gut says that it's high time for me to stop pussy-footing around. Rob and I need to deal with this head on instead of just hoping it will go away." She paused and added more softly, "You know I love that man to the moon. I just think we got out of our orbit and we need a jolt to get us back."

Kate smiled. "I really, really hope for the best

for you, Car. If there's anyone who can save a marriage, it's you."

"You know, not all relationships are meant to last," Caroline said, eyeing Kate above her glass. "Some are forever, and others are just for now."

Kate thought about that for a moment. She had always thought that her relationship with Zach would be forever, but maybe that was a false assumption. "I do think that Zach came into my life for a reason. Do you think that it wasn't meant to last?"

"Maybe, but only you can answer that. Some people change and evolve, some don't. What you wanted a year ago may not be what you want now." Caroline put her glass down before continuing. "After being with Rob for so many years, he's become like part of my skin. I owe it to both of us to try and make it work. But you and Zach? It might be too soon to tell."

Kate sat back and let her words sink in, feeling the reality settle into her gut.

Caroline picked the three espresso beans from her nearly empty glass and placed them one at a time on the white bar napkin. "Health. Wealth. Happiness." She looked up at Kate and said, "And you deserve all of these my dear."

Kate leaned over and gave her friend a long hug, holding her against her bosom, grateful for her words and their time together.

⇒ Twenty-Two ⇐

Chloe was sitting in the parking lot of H-E-B waiting for Chase to come when she finally saw his Bronco pull up next to her Prius. He jumped out and was at her passenger side in no time.

"Hey!" he said as he climbed in and had to move the chair back to fit his long legs.

"Are you ready for your personal vineyard tour?" Chloe asked as she watched him buckle his seatbelt.

"One hundred percent." He grinned at her and her heart skipped a beat as she looked into his sparkling eyes.

She quickly switched her gaze to the rear-view and began to back out of the parking spot. "Here we go!"

They drove for a while down 290 before finally turning off a county road that led further and further into the hills and away from the traffic.

She told Chase about Lillie and Paul, and baby Emma. How they were in France for a few months, but that she used to watch Emma to help out when she could.

"She gave me the gate code, so as long as it hasn't changed, we should be able to get in," Chloe said as she began to slow down before taking a sharp turn onto a steep driveway that went for a bit until it ended at a closed metal gate.

She pulled up to the keypad, rolling down

her window to reach out and press the numbers. After a second, a green light appeared and the gate slowly began to open.

"Rad!" Chase called out, and Chloe was relieved she would be able to show him the vineyard after all.

They pulled through the open gate, and as it slowly closed behind them, they made their way further down a long and winding gravel road until it split into a Y.

"That way is to Dennis' house, and this way is to his guest house where Lillie and Paul live." She pulled toward their house and the road curved until it came up to a sweet little guest house. She parked to the side and cut her ignition.

As they stepped out, she watched Chase take in the whole view.

"Dude, this is a huge ranch!" he said as he turned around.

"It's over fifty acres, I think?" Chloe said

and then grabbed her camera gear out of the backseat.

"Follow me!" She motioned to him and then headed back up the road towards Dennis' house. "Just beyond the house is the main vineyard."

Chase fell into step with her, and she loved how easy it was to be around him. Even with his large stride, she didn't feel like she had to rush to keep up the pace.

They saw a large old white-washed farmhouse up ahead, and as they hiked up the road a bit further, the rows and rows of vines appeared and stretched out far into the distance.

"Holy smokes, this place is so cool!" Chase picked up his pace a little and Chloe loved his excitement.

They went through a gate and she walked the rows with him, pointing out the different varietals, giving him details about the vines and the process.

Chase touched a cluster of merlot. "Can we eat these?"

She shrugged. "You could, but they are probably a little bitter. Still need some more time before they're ready for harvest."

Chloe reached out to move the canopy of green leaves away to inspect the clusters beneath, and her hand brushed against his tanned forearm. She pulled back, but not before catching a glint in his eye that made her stomach dance.

They made their way to the end of a row where there was a bench. They sat down and Chloe took her camera out of its bag. The air was still hot from the day, but as the sun was beginning to set, she could feel the coolness coming in and wondered if she should have brought her long-sleeved shirt.

"Wow, it's so freakin' peaceful out here. I could sit here every night. Not quite as nice as watching the ocean after a long day of riding waves, but pretty darn close." He stood up. "Okay if I walk around?"

"Sure. I'm going to start trying to get the perfect sunset shots." Chloe then made her way through the vines, aiming to capture the perfect combination of grape leaves and clusters with the orange and pink hues of light filtering through.

They weaved in and out of the rows for an hour, making their way back to the bench just as the sun was about to dip below the dark hills. They sat side by side in silence, listening to the repeated calls of the whippoorwill, and the dusk songs of cardinals calling out to their mates before heading to roost. Chloe heard a cow bray in the distance, and the wind picked up slightly, causing her to shiver.

"Cold?" Chase asked as he put his strong arm around her. Just the excitement of being so close to him again made her flush with warmth.

Chloe turned to look at him, letting her eye

wander up his chiseled jawline to his gorgeous eyes. They were so close, she could feel his breath tickle her forehead.

Just then, she heard the sound of a vehicle making its way slowly up the gravel driveway.

"Sshhh!" Chloe grabbed Chase and pulled him to the ground.

They watched pools of light get brighter until they saw the headlights pointing into their direction before pulling up towards the edge of the vineyard.

"I thought Dennis was gone," Chase whispered.

"He is," Chloe whispered back as she now shivered in fright thinking about the rumors of sabotage in the vineyards. Had the gate not closed behind them?

The car door slammed, but the headlights stayed on, blinding them. They could only make out a dark figure going into the vineyard.

They crept down against the end of the row

post to try to stay out of sight. Chloe got on her belly and instinctively held her camera between both hands.

The figure came down the rows until they reached theirs, and then slowly started walking towards them.

Chloe's heart quickened. What if they were discovered? Dennis wouldn't be back until the day after next, and no one else knew they were there.

She could feel Chase stiffen as if ready to pounce when the figure stopped halfway down the row. Then, they saw a large knife glisten in the light against the dark vines. The figure dropped down on one knee and began cutting the plastic tubing for the irrigation drip underneath the cordons.

Chloe realized that this was her chance: if she could catch the saboteur on camera, she could bring an end to the mystery.

She held her camera up and zoomed her

lens to get as close up as possible. Her hands were shaking as she watched two more pipes get cut, but all she could see through the lens was the dark figure against the brightness of the headlights.

Just then, the figure turned slightly towards the light and Chloe pressed her shutter, taking a rapid succession of photos, hoping that one of them might reveal the identity of the perpetrator.

The figure then got up and walked away from them and back down the row towards the fence, going through the gate and crossing in front of the headlights before getting in the driver's seat and backing out.

Chase and Chloe let out their breaths together, not realizing how long they'd been holding them. By now, it was pitch black, and all they could make out was a silhouette of a truck driving back down the gravel roadway.

Chase turned to Chloe. "Are you okay?"

She nodded, catching her breath again. "That was scary! To think that someone would come on the same night as us! What if they'd found us?"

"I was ready to defend us," Chase said, pumping up a bit to prove his worth.

Chloe's hands were still shaking as she looked down at her camera. "I just hope there's a clue here as to who it might be."

They leaned back against the bench and she began flipping through the images one by one. Most were just dark silhouettes with no distinguishable feature, except for one.

"Look! There's something shiny on his chest I think." Chloe zoomed the image closer and saw a shape that seemed familiar but couldn't quite place it. Something metal that had caught the light of the headlights just right.

Then, she gasped. "Chase! That's the same

Mason pin Dennis wears!" Chase leaned closer and could make out the G shape.

"But that makes no sense." She looked back at the photos, trying to make out more of the body shape. "It sure looks like it could be Dennis. But why would he sabotage his own vineyard?"

Chase ran his fingers through his hair perplexed, but relieved that they were out of danger. "C'mon. Let's get out of here before anything else happens."

She walked back down the row and asked Chase to use the flashlight on his phone to illuminate where the pipes had been cut so she could take pictures.

Then, fueled by adrenaline, they quickly made their way back to her Prius with Chase holding his iPhone out to illuminate their path.

Back at her dad's, Chloe stayed up late that night going through all the images trying to get more concrete evidence. She had opened them in Adobe Photoshop on her laptop and adjusted the contrast to try to bring out any distinguishing features.

There was a shot with the Mason pin on the jacket. Most of the others were too blurry. But there was one shot that showed the jawline and mustache. It was definitely Dennis.

Chloe sat back in her chair wondering what to do. She wanted to tell her dad right away, but didn't know how she would explain both Dennis, and Chase. She may have uncovered the person behind the trouble going on in Fredericksburg, and that could potentially help Peter and Chase. But that would reveal her secret relationship with Chase and what if her father didn't approve?

Then there were all the questions about Dennis. Was he behind sabotaging the labels? It still didn't explain to her why he would cut his own irrigation lines. Her head was swimming and she needed to tell someone. She thought of

Kate. She decided to call her first thing in the morning to get her advice. At the very least, she could help her figure out how to explain it to her father.

⇾ Twenty-Three ⇽

The next morning, Kate had just finished pressing her first cup of coffee into her mug when a text message from Chloe lit up her phone.

Hey! Can you call me this morning?

Kate instantly wondered if something was wrong because Chloe rarely called her directly, but instead always talked to Lillie. She pressed the button on her phone to call her.

"Hey." Chloe was half whispering.

"Are you okay?" Kate asked.

"Um, sort of? I really need your advice and was wondering if you could meet me before my shift today?" Chloe asked.

"Oh, sure! It's going to take me about 45 minutes to get there, but I can meet you by eleven if that works?"

"Perfect. Let's meet at Sunday Supply?" Chloe asked.

"Okay, I'll see you then." Kate said before hanging up wondering what sort of trouble Chloe needed help with. She was a very independent girl, with a strong sense of herself. Kate wondered if it had something to do with her father—was their relationship okay?

She swallowed down her coffee and tried to put her ruminations to rest. She would find out soon enough and was touched that Chloe would ask for her advice. With Lillie being out of the country, Kate missed having that sister time, and she sort of felt like Chloe was a little sister too. She hoped that it wasn't anything too bad, and that she would be able to help.

Just before 11am, Kate pulled her Durango into the parking lot at Sunday Supply. She saw Chloe's Prius already there, and she quickly made her way into the cafe. She placed her order at the front counter, and then made her way to the back where she saw Chloe sitting with a tall young man with red hair.

"Hi Kate!" She hugged her before turning to introduce Chase. "This is my friend, Chase."

Chase stood up and politely shook Kate's hand as Chloe beckoned her to take a seat.

"Nice to meet you, Chase." Kate was struck by how handsome the young man was, but a bit confused as to who he was.

Chloe filled her in quickly. "Kate, Chase and I have been friends all summer. Secret friends."

Kate raised her eyebrow. "Why secret?"

Chase and Chloe gave each other a knowing glance before she dove in. "Chase is Peter's son."

Kate's eyes opened wide. "Oh! Wow. Okay, I think I understand now."

Chase spoke up, "I've been helping my dad at his tasting room this summer, and I'm transferring from USC to UT this fall."

Chloe chimed in, "We just hit it off right away, we've been meeting every day for our pre-shift coffee. I just didn't know how to tell my dad because of the rift with Peter, and it doesn't seem that they will ever forgive each other."

Kate shook her head, taking it all in. "Yes, I can see how that would be tough. But, Chloe, I don't think keeping a secret from your dad is the right way to go about this. He's pretty understanding once he has all the information."

Right after the words left her mouth, Kate wondered if that was true for her and Zach as well. Would he really end up being understanding?

"I know, you're right. And I was trying to figure out a way to tell him before the summer ends. But I just wasn't sure of the right timing. And what if he doesn't approve?" Chloe squeaked out that last word as Chase gave her a sweet look that told Kate that their friendship may indeed be developing into something more.

"Okay, well, I can help with that—" Kate started to say, when Chloe cut her off.

"There's more." She pulled her laptop out of her bag and opened it on the table. She told Kate about how she and Chase went to the vineyard to take pictures when the stranger showed up after dark.

Chloe turned her laptop screen towards Kate as she leaned forward to get a better look. Kate had to agree—it was definitely Dennis. She'd recognize his distinct frame anywhere.

"But why would he do this? And do you think he's the one behind the other events?" Kate wondered out loud.

Chloe and Chase nodded together, both of their eyes pleading with Kate for help.

She sat for a moment taking it all in. Maybe it did make sense. She knew Dennis was passionately against what he called "outsiders." And she remembered the animosity between Dennis and Peter after their business deal went south.

"But, wasn't Dennis supposed to be in Lubbock yesterday?" Kate asked, trying to piece together the information.

"If everyone thought he was out of town, maybe they wouldn't suspect him," Chloe said.

Kate started to see the whole picture coming together, all the bits and pieces that didn't make sense separately, but together painted a picture that didn't bode well for Dennis. How would Zach deal with his partner going rogue?

"Okay, Chloe, let's go to the tasting room and tell your dad together," Kate said standing up.

Chloe put her laptop in her bag and then stood to hug Chase goodbye. He gave her a quick embrace, telling her to call him as soon as she could.

Kate shook the young man's hand, "Chase, it's really great to meet you. I'm sure we are going to work this all out." He shook hers back and responded with a wide grin. "Totally."

———

KATE AND CHLOE STOOD IN front of Winsome Winery tasting room and took a deep breath together before stepping inside.

Zach was taking the barstools off the bar top and turned around, surprised to see both of them. "Hey! I was expecting Chloe, but not you too," he said smiling at Kate before going over to give her a hug.

Kate pulled away and Zach saw the concern on both of their faces. "Is everything alright?"

Kate took the lead. "We have something to tell you and think you'd better sit down for this." She pointed to one of the tables and they took a seat.

Zach was a bit perplexed, immediately

jumping into father mode. "Chloe, are you in trouble?"

Chloe shook her head and looked at Kate with pleading eyes.

"There's no easy way to say it, Chloe. I think you need to tell your dad the entire story." Kate encouraged her.

Chloe took a deep breath and then dove in. She told her dad about meeting Chase at Walmart, and how they were meeting in secret all summer, about the letter, and the tampering at the labeling facility, and then finally about last night's adventure.

Chloe pulled out her laptop and showed him the pictures.

Zach shifted in his seat taking it all in. His face was unreadable, and Kate knew he had just switched into his doctor role, not giving away any emotion but instead coming up with the most pragmatic solution. Yet, a twitch in his jaw betrayed his cool exterior.

He cleared his throat and finally spoke. "Why do I feel like I'm the last one to know anything?"

Kate could feel his frustration and knew it was about more than what Chloe had just revealed.

He then caught himself and softened. "Chloe, I'm disappointed in you. Why didn't you feel like you could tell me about Chase?"

Chloe's eyes were glassy as she swallowed hard. "Dad, I know your issue with Peter and I was so scared that you'd be upset with me."

He shook his head and stood up to go to her. He pulled her into a long hug that brought tears to Kate's eyes at how openly loving he was to her.

"You're my daughter. I will always want what's best for you." He pulled back and wiped a tear from her cheek. "That business with Peter is between us. It has nothing to do with you and Chase. Do you understand?"

Chloe shook her head and wiped the tears of relief that fell down her sweet face.

"Listen, you're a grown woman now. You're going to make your own choices, and I don't want you to ever keep anything from me again, okay?" He got her to grin by pinching her cheek and they hugged again.

He sat down and pointed to the laptop. "This whole thing has gotten out of control, and I'm going to handle this with Dennis." He then asked his daughter, "Can you send those photos to my email?" She nodded and turned her laptop around to do just that.

He turned to Kate. "Thank you for helping out."

Kate nodded. "Of course. But, how are you going to deal with Dennis?" She was worried he'd lose his friend and partner.

"Don't you worry. I'll figure something out." His jaw was tense again and she could only imagine the anger he felt at having to confront him.

"Chloe, it's time to open," he said and stood up signaling the end of the conversation.

Kate stood as well, and Chloe came around to Kate and gave her a big hug. "Thank you!"

Kate smiled and was glad that Chloe's secret was out for good.

She turned to Zach and he gave her a quick hug and a peck on the cheek before pulling away quickly. She wondered if he still hadn't forgiven her for her own secret about the contract.

She brushed it off, realizing he had just taken in a lot of information and had a difficult task ahead of him.

"Give me a call when you can, and good luck with Dennis," she said before turning around to leave.

"Kate," he called after her.

She turned back around to face him.

"Thank you."

She nodded in appreciation, but there was something inside her that felt a shift in their usual intimacy.

⇾ Twenty-Four ⇽

That evening after the tasting room was closed and Chloe had left to go back to the house, Zach texted Dennis.

Are you back from Lubbock?

He waited for a moment and then saw the three animated dots as Dennis typed his reply.

Yessir.

Can you meet me at the tasting room? I need to talk.

Dennis replied a brief moment later, *You bet.*

Zach clicked his phone off and uncorked a bottle to pour himself a glass of Mourvédre. He sat at the bar swirling the base of the glass between his fingers on the bar top, watching the swirling motion hypnotically.

It had been a busy day, but the thoughts of everything that had surfaced that morning had hummed in the background as he tried to sort through it. The look on his daughter's face when she thought she had let him down nearly broke his heart. It only takes moments like those to create division, and he was grateful that she was finally forced to tell him her secret. He also worried that he hadn't done a good enough job raising her if she was that nervous about telling him.

He took a sip, letting the smooth wine soothe his throat. He shook it off. It would probably have been different had it not involved his ex-business partner and he took full responsibility for his part in the rift between them. He would have to make a point to talk to Peter and bury that hatchet once and for all if Chloe was to have a future with his son.

Then, he thought about Kate. He wanted so badly to be supportive of her, and was so impressed with her ability to write. When he met her, he knew she would be wildly successful as an author, but he sort of assumed that they would be living together in the Hill Country. It wasn't just the fact that she was going on a year-long book tour, but the fact that she made that decision without even consulting him. Why did she keep that a secret from him as well? He felt left out and confused as to whether she even wanted to be with him at all, and that made him even more concerned for their future.

Just then, the door opened and Dennis walked in confidently, tipping his hat to Zach and saddled up next to him at the bar.

Zach looked at his friend and business partner still partially in disbelief. Then he saw the same metallic G pin on his chest and realized that he had no choice but to confront him. "How was your trip?"

Dennis took his hat off lay it on the bar top. "It was great. Our block is growing well, and with the rain they've had this year, I think we'll have increased yield."

Zach's jaw twitched as he looked at his partner straight in the face. "Dennis. I need to ask you something."

Dennis grew serious. "Shoot."

Zach took a deep breath and then let it out. "Are you behind what's been going on around town?"

Dennis' eyebrows shot up. "Are you talking about me getting the other growers together to protect our rights? You bet! We sent letters out to try and persuade them to stay out."

"No." Zach was firm. "I'm talking about more than the letter. I'm talking about you sabotaging things to drive out the new vineyards and tasting rooms."

Dennis nervously fingered the edges of his mustache as his eyes stayed locked on his partner's.

"I'm not sure what you mean."

Zach sat up straight, getting more agitated. "I mean, tampering with the label machine at the production facility, for instance."

Zach was sure he saw Dennis' eyes flicker for a moment before he said, "Now, that's just a coincidence."

Zach pulled his phone out of his pocket and opened Chloe's incriminating picture.

He shoved it in Dennis' face. "And this? Is this a coincidence too?"

Dennis' face went white as he tried to recover. "I can explain—"

Zach pounded his hand on the bar top spilling his wine. "Damnit, Dennis. Enough!"

He could feel the heat burning his cheeks and behind his collar as he confronted Dennis.

"Okay, okay. You're right. I might have taken things a bit far," Dennis began.

Zach stood up and began pacing in the room. "Too far?! Dennis, what the hell! I know you've had this vendetta building for a while against outsiders coming in. And the business with Peter didn't help. But, there is no 'us' and 'them', we're all in this together!" Zach motioned a large circle in the air.

Dennis was silent as stone while Zach continued.

"All this crap about building walls and separating us, and who belongs and who doesn't is a load of horseshit and you know it!" Zach continued. "And, to be honest, I can't even believe that you would stoop so low as to incite more animosity through sabotage." Zach caught his breath and then moved towards Dennis, looking him straight in the eye.

"More than anything, I'm disappointed because you're not the man I thought you were. All this time I thought you were this God-fearing Christian, upstanding citizen, someone I could depend on, and then you go and do this?"

Zach paused and then asked point blank, "Do I even know you anymore?"

Dennis gripped the rail on the bar top, "You don't understand. This is *my* land, *my* heritage. I can't stand by and watch it get ruined because of someone else's greed."

"So that means you can sabotage and threaten, and spread rumors? How is that any better?"

Dennis and Zach stared at each other as the room suddenly became very quiet. Zach still felt the rage pulsing throughout his body, and he struggled to maintain a level head.

"So, you were behind everything?"

Dennis' mustache twitched slightly.

"The tampered barrels at Slate Theory too?"

"No, sir." Dennis said quickly. "I take full responsibility for bringing the growers together, and the letters, and I did mess with the labeling machine, but that wasn't anything too expensive to fix." He was firm. "I had no part in what happened at Slate. That was a disgruntled worker… but, I did use it to my advantage."

Zach looked at his face and felt like he was being sincere, but still wasn't sure. How could he have misjudged his friend and partner through all of this? He felt betrayed and confused as to whether they could move forward.

"You know I've put everything into this tasting room. This dream. I can't lose it now." Zach pointed to his partner. "I need you to be in this with me, not against me."

Dennis looked down as if praying. "Maybe I got carried away with it all," he began. "I never fully forgave Peter for what he did to us. That was the deepest insult to me and to you.

Then, all the other wineries and tasting rooms kept coming in, and the community started to feel the pain, I just wanted to do something to fix it."

Zach sat back down across from him. "But, Dennis, we can't change all of that, it's inevitable."

Dennis shook his head, "I'm not so sure about that."

Zach cleared his throat, still trying to understand. "I get why you would mess with Peter's production, but why our irrigation system?"

Dennis wiped his forehead. "Ah, hell. The other growers weren't totally on board, they thought we could handle the water issue over time with more regulations and fewer permits. I needed to add more fuel to the fire, and I figured I could make it look like someone tampered with our vines and then fix it easily enough after. Since I was supposed to be in Lubbock,

I thought I wouldn't get caught. I had no idea your daughter would be out there."

"Be glad she was." Zach said. "If your rumor had gotten out, you would be making things a hell of a lot worse for others. You might have even incited violence."

Dennis was silent for a moment, and Zach could hear the hum of the overhead fan moving the air softly above them.

"She wasn't alone."

Dennis raised an eyebrow.

"She was with Peter's son."

Dennis' eyes clouded briefly as he took in this information.

"My daughter's happiness means even more to me than this tasting room," Zach said. "If you can't work with me on this, and make amends, then I will have to reconsider this whole partnership," Zach said.

Dennis suddenly stood, grabbed his hat off the bar top and then turned to Zach. Their eyes locked and in that moment Zach wasn't sure if anything he'd said had made a difference. Dennis turned to leave and the door shut firmly behind him.

Twenty-Five

Early the next morning, Dennis was parked in front of the All Points Between tasting room. He had hardly slept that night after Zach's come to Jesus talk, and he was conflicted. His hatred towards Peter had grown so deep that he wasn't sure he could swallow his pride and get over it.

Peter represented everything he despised—from the way he dressed, to his obnoxious confidence. He didn't belong in the Hill

Country. But Dennis' efforts to change that had backfired, and instead he was facing an even greater loss of his partnership and friendship with Zach.

He saw Peter walking up the sidewalk and he got out of his truck to approach him. "Peter."

Peter stopped short, suspicious of his intention. "Dennis."

"I'd like a word with you if that's alright," Dennis said as politely as he could muster.

"Okay..." Peter eyed him again before turning to unlock the front door, leaving it open for him to follow.

He flipped on lights and then turned around a safe distance from Dennis. "Alright, what's on your mind? And if you're here to tell me to leave, you'd better just turn right back around. We're not going anywhere, and I have lawyers ready to back us up on that."

Dennis clenched his jaw. "You can leave the

lawyers out of this. We handle things differently around here."

"Yeah, I see that," Peter said as he stood taller. "You and your vigilante justice."

"That's right. We demand justice and respect. *You're* the outsider here."

"It's a free country."

The two men faced off. Dennis' hands twitched at his sides.

"I'm not here to fight with you, Peter," Dennis finally said.

Peter shifted his stance. "Okay, then why are you here?"

Dennis continued begrudgingly, "I'm here to make amends. On behalf of Zach."

Peter regarded him suspiciously. "I'm listening."

"I'm behind the letter that you got from the committee, and I'm meeting with them today to tell them everything, to get them to back down." he started.

"Everything? What about my window?" Peter demanded as he pointed to the temporary piece of plywood in place.

Dennis struggled. As much as he had wanted to punish Peter and send him packing, he no longer had the upper hand and that felt extremely uncomfortable. He thought again of Zach and knew that this was the honorable thing to do.

"I don't know about your window. But, I was the one who tampered with your labels. And, I fully intend to make amends for that." Dennis stated.

"I figured you were behind that. What the hell were you thinking? That by messing with my business you'd scare me off?" Peter's voice began to rise.

Dennis couldn't hold back, "The same way you screwed our business over last year by shipping your bullshit California wine to our one hundred percent Texan tasting room. That wasn't an easy mess to fix. We almost didn't open at all."

The muscle in Dennis' jaw twitched as he waited for Peter's response.

"That was the right business decision in terms of the ROI," Peter stated.

"Well, I don't give a shit about your ROI. We care more about preserving the history and legacy of this land and the fruit from it than any bottom line." Dennis responded.

Just then, Chase came in through the front door. His eyes flew wide open when he saw the men standing there as though they were about to fight—Peter in his yellow polo shirt, pleated khaki shorts, and Italian loafers; Dennis in his signature Wranglers, western snap button shirt, and square-toed work boots.

"Uh, is everything okay here?" He walked up next to his father.

"We're fine, son." Peter said not taking his eyes off Dennis.

After a long moment, he stepped forward with his hand outstretched. "Let's just call it even, alright?"

Dennis nodded and met him in the middle to shake on it.

"It's more than just business now." He motioned to Chase before releasing the handshake and walking out the door.

"Whoa, that was intense!" Chase said after Dennis left.

"Let's just say that a little karma came back around," Peter said, putting a hand on Chase's shoulder. "It's all going to be fine now. But what was he talking about, that this is 'more than business'?" Peter turned to his son.

"Uh, yeah. So, we need to talk," Chase said before telling him about Chloe and their secret meetings, budding friendship, and the vineyard tour.

"Is it serious?" Peter asked.

"Dad, I really like her. And it was so cool

to be out in the vineyard, watching her take photos. Like, her stuff would look awesome in here. She showed me how this is so much more than just wine. It's the land, and everything..." he trailed off.

Peter watched his son and realized he was smitten, and knew that he wasn't going to be able to brush this off. Whatever had bloomed this summer between him and Chloe was indeed something more. He wouldn't stand in the way of that. He knew right then that he needed to figure out how to make amends with Zach.

⋙Twenty-Six⋘

Kate had finally finished her spreadsheet with all the logistics for her book tour. Hundreds of rows of cities, RV parks, reservation confirmations, Target stores, and business contacts. She also had plugged in the routes to each destination in RVTripWizard, the waypoints connected by jagged lines that took her along the highways and byways across the country.

She attached both to an email to Margaret, and then pressed send. Blowing out a breath, a mixture of excitement and fear washed over her. It was now real. She was really going on this year-long tour to promote her latest book in less than a month. She sat back in her Airstream dinette and wondered what she was doing. Was this the right decision? What if she got tired of being on the road? What if she hated it?

Her thoughts turned to her greatest fear: what if she lost Zach?

Ever since she told him she had agreed to go, their conversations weren't the same. He had been busy with the winery, and she had focused on coordinating logistics. They exchanged short texts, and brief calls, but they never really dug into the heart of the matter.

She knew that with Chloe's secret, and Dennis' lies, that Zach had reached his limit. Kate hated that she had also pushed him to that edge. The people-pleasing part of her wanted to make it right, to cancel her plans, move in with him, and give him everything he wanted to be happy.

She sighed. That was the old Kate. The one who married impulsively, and jumped through hoops and contorted herself to try adhere to someone else's wishes, ultimately sabotaging her own happiness in the process.

Her gut was firm. She owed it to herself to do this tour, to go all in on her writing, her books, her dreams, her future. Whether that future would include Zach, she'd have to wait to find out.

Her phone buzzed, and she saw Caroline's face pop up on the screen.

"Hello, friend!"

"Well, a howdy-do to you too, my dear!" Caroline was chipper on the other end, making Kate smile.

"How are things? Are you okay?" Kate ventured.

"Oh, darlin', I'm fine as frog hair and excited as a hog in heat!" Caroline laughed.

"Tell me!" Kate put her phone down on the dinette table and pressed the speaker button so that Caroline's voice filled up the trailer.

"Well, I think my trip to your slice of paradise did the trick," Caroline began. "That time away from Rob did something. I came back and he had fixed things around the house that he had been putting off for years. He even cleaned out his old crap from the garage."

"Wow! So, he must have missed you?"

"I do declare!" Caroline continued. "I got back home, opened up one of those fabulous bottles of wine we picked up from Adega Vinho, I plopped two glasses down, and told him, 'We aren't going out of this house until we finish this bottle and figure out our situation once and for all.'"

"What did he say?"

"Well, let's just say we went through a few

more bottles, and it was a very, very late night. But we were finally able to get some things off our chests and out in the open." Caroline paused to catch her breath. "And you know what? Neither of us want to separate. We just had so many misunderstandings built up over so much time that we didn't know how to get through it all and really tell each other what we needed."

"And what do you both need?" For a moment, Kate half-regretted that she couldn't have had the same outcome with her own marriage. What if her ex-husband had actually cared about her needs? She quickly dismissed the thought.

"A good 'ol fashioned adventure!" Caroline laughed. "We realized that we hadn't taken a trip, just the two of us, for over ten years. Can you even imagine?"

"Wow! That is a long time. Where are you going to go?"

"Well, we've always wanted to tour the wine country in France, and just never felt we could be away from the boys for that long. Now that's changed. We need to put ourselves and our relationship first, because, after all, we came first."

Kate laughed. "Indeed. Wow, France." She instantly thought of Lillie. "Will you visit Burgundy?"

"Oui! We rang up Lillie and chatted with Martine and Didier and will be staying at their estate for a week!" Caroline could hardly contain her excitement.

"Fantastic! Oh, Car, I'm so happy for you both. A romantic get-away in France, and you know they will spoil you rotten!"

"I have absolutely no doubt!" Caroline practically squealed. "Listen, enough about me, how's my favorite author?"

Kate filled her in on the book tour logistics, and all the planning. "So, I guess I'm ready?"

"Now, you'll be coming to Pensacola in about

four months, right? So, for sure, we'll see you then," Caroline said.

"I'd love that. I'm really not sure what to expect from all of this, and seeing a familiar face will be more than welcome..." she trailed off as she again wondered about the future.

Just then, she saw a text message notification pop up on her phone: *Harvest on Friday!*

"Oh! Car, it looks like the merlot grapes are ready and we'll be harvesting later this week!" Kate was giddy from the idea of finally getting to help hand-pick the first batch of grapes for Zach's winery.

"Good for Dr. Wine! And just in time before you leave!" Caroline gushed.

"The perfect Texas wine send-off ...I hope?" Kate said.

"Now, gurl, you know everything will work out as its meant to. You have a fabulous future ahead of you—don't lose sight of that, alright?" Caroline said.

"Thanks, Car. I'll keep you posted."

"And, send pics," Caroline added before disconnecting.

Kate got up and stretched. She had a few days to get all her provisions together before hitching up and heading out. She still had so many questions about where she stood with Zach, but hoped that they would find time to open a bottle of their own wine and clear the air. Maybe after harvest.

She texted Zach back: *Count me in!*

⇝ Twenty-Seven ⇜

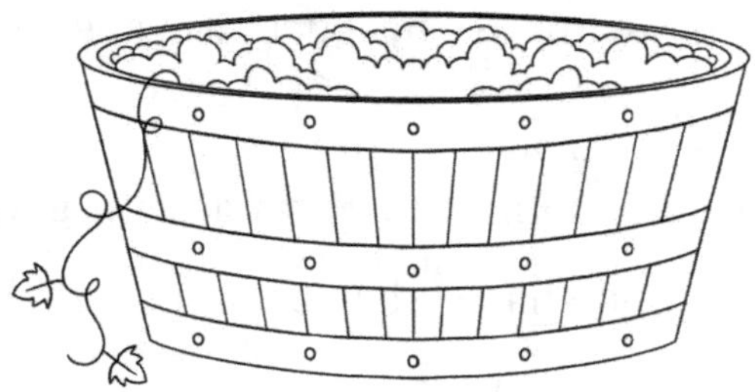

It was still dark when Zach showed up to the vineyard. Dennis was already setting up the tables under the metal outbuilding. Zach parked his car against the fence and then made his way over to him.

"Dennis," Zach said as he came closer.

"Partner," Dennis said and reached out to shake his hand.

Zach had made his position with Dennis clear, but they hadn't talked much since that heated conversation in the tasting room. Zach hoped he had done the right thing.

"Can we talk?" Zach asked.

"Yessir," Dennis stood tall facing him, bugs dancing underneath the outdoor lights.

"I just want to be sure we are good?" Zach asked.

"You have nothing to worry about. I gave you my word, and I have taken care of everything," Dennis said solemnly.

Zach breathed a sigh of relief. "That's good to hear. So, the business with that committee is done?"

"Yessir. There won't be any more letters."

"And, the business with Peter?"

"All handled. We've arrived at a truce of sorts," Dennis said as he leaned against one of the metal support beams.

"Good," Zach said, not sure whether he wanted to know the details.

"I owe you an apology," Dennis said.

Zach looked over at his friend and partner, and he shook his head. "No, you don't. I'm just glad that we could get past this and focus on the success of our business."

"Zach, I mean it: I'm sorry for being so short-sighted that I was willing to jeopardize our friendship and partnership." He looked out over the vines for a moment and then back to Zach. "I'm grateful for your forgiveness."

Zach stood up and approached him. "I couldn't do this without you, and you know that. And you're a good man, Dennis. This was just a hiccup, and I'm glad we can move forward," he said and pulled him into a big bear hug.

KATE WOUND HER WAY DOWN 290 towards the vineyard. Her bright headlights navigated each turn in the road, illuminating the dormant wineries and vines along the way. She relished traveling at this time because the normal deluge of tourist traffic was absent and she could drive with ease and take in the views. Her only concern was the axis deer that liked to feed early mornings, so she kept an eye out along the sides of the highway and flicked her high beam on when there were no oncoming vehicles.

Kate was nervous, this being her first time harvesting. She was told to wear comfortable clothes and plenty of sunscreen. Even though they were starting right before dawn, the temperature was already warming up. She wore her convertible REI zipper parachute pants so she could turn them into shorts when needed. She had her most comfortable sneakers on, a bright red bandana around her neck, and a big sun hat for later in the day.

She pulled up to Dennis' gate and punched the code Zach had given her before slowly making her way up the gravel drive. She saw a bunch of cars and trucks of volunteers parked along the fence line to the vineyard and shivered in delight as she could make out the lush vines in the distance.

She pulled into an open spot next to a black Chevy Silverado and cut her engine. Stepping out, she breathed in the early morning air, the smells of limestone and cedar. Kate shoved her water bottle, sunscreen, and ChapStick into her backpack, then grabbed her sun hat and made her way to meet the others by the fence gate.

There were fifteen or so people standing around, getting acquainted and sipping on their YETIs filled with coffee. Most of them were members of the wine club volunteering to help with the harvest in exchange for a couple bottles of wine and lunch.

Kate introduced herself to a few of them, then she looked around and finally saw Zach walking up carrying orange Home Depot buckets sandwiched together. She waved, and he gave her a nod and grin before passing out the buckets to the members.

Chloe beckoned to her, and Kate went over and gave her a big hug. "How is everything?" Kate asked her.

"OMG. Like so much better now." Chloe grinned, pulling her aside. "Chase told me that Dennis went over to make amends with Peter."

"What? That's amazing." Kate said, wondering how hard that must have been for Dennis considering all the bad blood between them. While she didn't approve of the measures he took, she understood his motivation, trying to preserve the Hill Country. She admired the fact that although he was stubborn in his beliefs, that he was able to find a way to compromise.

"And the best part? Chase and I are no longer sneaking around!" Chloe said with relief.

"I'm so glad for you both!" Kate said, feeling genuinely pleased that they had a shot at making it work.

Zach came over and gave Kate a side hug. "I'm glad you're here."

She looked up at him, a hitch in her throat as she longed to kiss him but wasn't sure she still could.

"I've got to get everyone organized, but I'd love if you stuck around later so we can talk?" he asked.

"Of course. I'd like that." She felt a flutter in her stomach as he squeezed her shoulders once more.

She saw Dennis come up behind Zach.

"Kate, it's good to see you," he said in his usual polite manner and gave her a bear hug. She squeezed him back hard, wanting him to know that she forgave him. "It's really good to see you too." He pulled away and nodded to her as if he understood.

"Oh my gosh, they came!" Chloe squealed and Kate turned to see Chase and his father walking towards the gate.

Chloe ran over to meet Chase, giving him a hug, and escorting them inside to where Zach, Dennis, and Kate were standing.

"Peter, I wasn't expecting to see you," Zach said and stretched out his hand.

Peter shook it firmly. "I figured it was about time I got my hands dirty and found out what this Texas wine fuss is all about."

He then reached out to shake Dennis' hand and they nodded to each other. Kate watched and realized that the possibility of a real truce was becoming a reality.

"Dad, this is Chase!" Chloe said.

"It's a pleasure to meet you, Chase," Zach said. "Finally."

Chase laughed and shook his hand enthusiastically.

"Hey, Chase," Kate said, and then turned to his father, "Peter, it's good to see you as well."

"We'd better get started. We've got a lot to

pick before it gets too hot," Dennis said and then began organizing the volunteers, handing out the shears for clipping, and moving everyone to the end posts.

Chloe grabbed Chase's arm and took him to one end post. "Let's work this row," she said and then turned over a bucket to sit on, and he did the same. "You have to get low to really see and cut all the grapes."

"Dude, they're so much bigger than when we saw them just a few weeks ago," Chase marveled at the fruit.

"Yeah, don't they look great?" Chloe said.

Zach grabbed a bucket and motioned for Kate to follow him. He set her up at the end of an empty row, and then turned one bucket over for her to sit. "Try to get all the clusters in a section and then move down the row," he said. "You can put them in this bucket." He motioned to another empty bucket next to her. "Don't worry too much if you get some leaves in there because the de-stemmer will filter all that out."

Kate looked at the luscious grapes and watched as he clipped a few from the cordon. She then clipped her first big cluster and held it in her hand. It was a gorgeous shade of bluish purple. "They're so heavy!" she exclaimed as she turned to Zach.

"Bursting with our future wine," he said. For a moment she felt a closeness with him again and wished that they were alone.

He turned back to the vines. "Merlot grapes are tricky as they like to wrap themselves around the wires. Just do your best to cut around them and pull them out." He pointed out the challenging areas. "That's why we have to hand-harvest these. They just don't do well with the machines."

A volunteer called out for another bucket, and he patted her back gently and took off down the row. Kate missed him immediately and took a deep breath before getting back to work. She saw that some volunteers wore gloves, but she liked to feel the texture of the vines and the smoothness of the taught skin on the grapes. There were so many that it wasn't long before her bucket was full and she was calling out for another.

Dennis drove the skid-steer up the row, taking the full buckets from her and the other volunteers, replacing them with empties. He then took the grapes up to the de-stemmer where their winemaker, Leah, was supervising the process.

The sun was climbing quickly, and it wasn't long before Kate zipped off her pant legs, turning them into shorts. She took the sunscreen out of her bag and sprayed her legs before adjusting her hat and continuing to work.

She listened to the other volunteers talk about this and that. They were mostly older, retired couples and people who had lived in the community a long time. Many of them went to the same churches and gathered for events on a regular basis.

Kate wondered about whether she would ever be like that again—part of a community. She clipped some leaves away to expose another beautifully full cluster and began cutting it away carefully from the hardened vines. There was a part of her that longed for that sense of community and belonging. It seemed like human nature. But she knew she was different.

She wasn't married, and didn't have children. It was one of the first things people asked her when they met: where she was from, who her husband was, did she have kids. Oh, and in the South? Which church she belonged to.

Kate let her mind wander as she continued down the row filling up the bucket. She wiped a trickle of perspiration from her forehead with her bandana.

She had gotten used to explaining her solo

life as an author, and she felt like she had been accepted in the community in many ways. Yet, she wasn't fully an insider.

Moving in with Zach and making their relationship more permanent would secure her place in this community and give her that sense of belonging she had always longed for.

She clipped some dried up dead fruit off the cluster before tossing it in the bucket. But had those feelings, those desires to belong, changed?

She stood up and stretched her back, shielding her eyes from the sun to look around at the other rows before looking at her own. She'd made it halfway down her row already and felt extremely proud of what she had accomplished with her own hands.

Kate fetched her water bottle and took a long drink, letting the cold refresh her from the inside. She had one thought as she re-capped the bottle: could she belong and be free at the same time?

⇾ Twenty-Eight ⇽

Chloe and Chase worked side by side in the sun for hours and Chloe was thrilled that their friendship was finally out in the open. She liked watching his long fingers carefully unwrap the clusters from the wire and then cut them free.

"You're getting really good at that," she said as she dropped another of her clusters into the bucket.

"It's not too hard once you get the hang of

it." He grinned at her, and then cut some of the larger grape leaves away to expose more fruit.

"So, you're all set for UT this fall?" Chloe asked.

"Yup. Far as I know. All the paperwork has gone through, and I found a sweet room to rent not far from campus."

"That's great!" Chloe was glad that they would still be able to spend time together after the summer's end.

It was getting hotter, and they heard someone call for lunch. Many of the volunteers began to head up towards the patio to finish for the day.

"I'm good for a little longer," Chase said. "How about you?"

"Yeah, me too."

They continued to work the row until they got to the far end and they fought playfully over the last cluster.

"Okay, here, I'll hold, you cut." Chase laughed as they worked together.

Chloe realized how close they had gotten in a very short amount of time. They were practically finishing each other's sentences and just seemed so in tune.

She grabbed the cluster of grapes and pulled one off, rubbing the tough skin between her forefingers and then holding it out to him. "Wanna taste?"

He leaned towards her fingers and gently took the full grape into his mouth, biting down with bright eyes. "Mmm ...it's sort of tart!"

He didn't pull away.

Instead, he pulled a grape off, and after cleaning off the surface, held it up in front of his face for her.

Her stomach danced as she looked into his green eyes and let him place it against her soft lips. She bit down, chewing slowly, letting the juice glide down her throat, never once dropping his gaze.

He then leaned all the way in and pressed his

sun-kissed warm lips against hers as they kissed for the first time. Chloe tasted the salty-sweetness on his tongue and their lips fit together like perfect pillows.

They pulled away slightly and she brushed a long strand of his red hair away from his face, letting her finger slowly trace his jaw line.

"That was totally worth the wait," he said.

Chloe giggled. "It's about time!"

He pulled her into a big bear hug and didn't let go.

⇒ Twenty-Nine ⇐

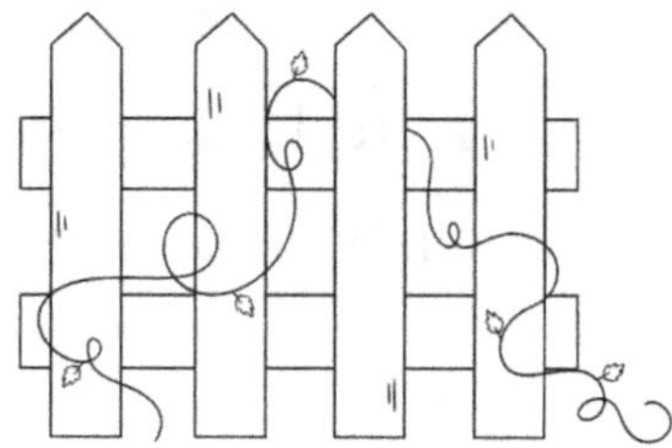

It was noon, and the midday sun was burning hot on the vines. The volunteers began to seek shelter inside Dennis' metal outbuilding and someone arrived with lunch and refreshments.

Kate finished up her last bucket and then joined the others as well, grabbing another bottle of water to rehydrate.

"That's it for the day, folks," Dennis said. "We'll continue tomorrow morning to get the last four rows, so anyone who'd like to join us, please do."

Kate walked up to the makeshift tables and was grabbing a fresh sandwich from the tray when a member came up with a bottle of wine and a plastic cup. She poured a cup for Kate and said, "This is the real reason we help out." She winked and then walked over to pour the next glass.

Kate appreciated the gesture and then looked around to find a place to eat. She spied an empty loveseat up on Dennis' porch and made her way there. As she did, she saw Chloe and Chase still out in the vines. The two of them made a precious picture.

Kate settled back on the patio and was surprised at how tired she was from just four hours of work. She rubbed her lower back and then took a long sip of wine, hoping it would help ease the pain.

She watched everyone at a distance

enjoying their wine and fellowship, but felt more comfortable relaxing by herself for the moment. She ate her lunch and watched as the volunteers began to trickle out one by one.

Zach appeared with a bottle and took a seat next to her.

"How'd we do?" Kate asked as she let him refill her cup.

"It looks really good. Leah is really excited about this batch," he said, leaning back into his chair.

Kate loved his proximity to her, but wasn't sure how to bridge the gap. Time was running out though, with her leaving in a few days. She needed to know where they stood.

"Kate..." Zach started. "Are you ready for your trip?"

"Pretty much. I have everything planned out, and have most of my provisions packed up." Kate felt her throat dry and took another sip of wine.

Zach looked at her. "I am really happy for you, you know that, right?"

"Of course." Kate waited for the but.

"I've thought about everything long and hard, and with everything that's happened this summer—with all the secrets and lies—I realized that I also need to be brutally clear about what I need." He looked at her. "What I want."

Kate felt a lump in her throat and dreaded what he was about to say.

"Zach, I do want the best for you. I really do—"

He didn't let her finish. "I know that. I just know myself, and I can't do a long distance relationship. Not for a year."

Kate felt herself deflate as her greatest fear became reality, and her eyes teared up.

"I'm sorry. I really am." he said as he leaned towards her to try and console her, as she pulled away.

Kate wiped the hot tears off her cheeks. "I

don't understand why? It's only one year, and it's not like we spend time together every day now anyway?"

"I wish we could."

Kate swallowed hard as Zach leaned back in his seat. "You see, it's not just you. It goes back to the reason I got divorced."

Kate took a sip of wine to ease the lump in her throat as he continued.

"When Chloe's mom and I first married, we were both very ambitious. I was in medical school and she was working up the ranks in real estate in Boston. We had Chloe and stayed busy with separate schedules—mostly communicating when we needed to coordinate gymnastics pickups or ride-shares."

He looked up to be sure Kate was still listening before continuing. "Near the end, as Chloe got older, I hoped we would slow down a bit and spend more time together. When I brought that up to her, she told me that she loved her life—her freedom, as she called it. And she had no intention of changing."

Kate took it all in and the realization hit her how in some ways she was very similar to his ex-wife. "But I thought you didn't have an issue with ambition? I thought you were okay with my goals and dreams?"

"I am. But I think that I didn't realize until just now how much I don't want our relationship to end up on that same path. I regret now that I didn't try harder—that I let our closeness slip away." He looked into her eyes. "I moved down here to the Hill Country to open this winery, but also to settle down with someone. I want a partner I can wake up with each morning, share everything together, and go to bed at night in each other's arms."

Kate swallowed hard as she realized that this was something she was not prepared to do now, or maybe ever. What he said sounded lovely for someone, but Kate knew that deep down inside, she was still restless and needed more adventure. She wasn't convinced yet that the Hill Country was where she wanted to stay.

"I get it now. It's okay..."

"No. It isn't," he said, and pulled her close for a long hug.

She leaned into him, breathing in his after-shave, and let out her tears against his firm chest.

After a while, she pulled away and they sat back against each other, her head against his shoulder.

"Oh, Zach. I'm sorry. I really am." She sniffled and pulled a tissue out of her pocket.

"Don't be," he said, pulling her closer. "You are one of the best things to happen to me, Kate. I mean that." He looked down at her. "I love you, Kate."

"I love you too," she said, and tucked herself against his chest as he rested his chin on top of her head. He took a deep breath, and she rose and fell with him.

A beeping in the driveway caught their attention and Kate raised her head to see what the commotion was. Zach stood up to get a better look. "Is that Lillie and Paul?"

Kate jumped up to see her dear sister, brother-in-law, and baby niece pulling up to park at the fence line. She wiped her cheeks and quickly made her way to meet them, grateful for the distraction from what seemed to be the end of her relationship with Zach.

"Sis!" she exclaimed as she met Lillie at the passenger side of the car.

Lillie got out of the car looking even more tanned and beautiful than before she left at the beginning of summer. Her chic bob had grown out a bit, but her black hair still sharply accented her gorgeous blue eyes.

"We're back!" Lillie hugged her hard, and Kate felt the love of her sister fill the crack in her heart that was growing larger.

"I didn't know you were coming back early,"

Kate said breathlessly, as she wiped tears of joy from her eyes.

"It was a surprise! I wanted to see you before you left on your book tour, so we made the change a few weeks ago," Lillie said. "And, apparently, just in time for harvest?" She motioned to all the orange buckets strewn about the vineyard.

"Yes, we just did the first day of merlot!" Kate was beyond happy to see her sister, then she watched Paul pull Emma out of the car seat in back and come around to her side of the car.

"Emma!" Kate exclaimed. "Welcome home, Paul," she gave him a half hug with Emma sandwiched between, her cute chubby cheeks full of life and joy. The baby squealed with delight, grabbing at Kate's bandana and smiling a wide toothless grin.

"Okay, can we start with: who's the hot guy Chloe's making out with in the vineyard?" Lillie asked as she playfully nudged Kate.

"That is a long, but really good story. And she should probably tell you herself," Kate said. "I'm so glad I get to see you before I leave."

"Same. We're going to get unpacked and then how about we head to dinner, just you and I?" Lillie asked to Kate's delight.

"I'd love that." She realized that sometimes a sister just knows exactly the right things to say at the right time. Sisters, and good friends. Kate realized she would be leaning into those relationships more over the next year, and although the thought scared her—not having Zach to reassure her and be her support—she knew that she would be alright. In time.

<h1 style="text-align:center">⇢ Thirty ⇤</h1>

Kate was putting the last load of provisions in her Airstream preparing to leave that morning. The air was warm but dry, and the sun was just beginning to gain traction, slowly climbing the big blue sky.

She had her red bandana wrapped around her blond hair to keep it from flying around in the breeze. She was wearing her favorite pair of comfortable blue overall-shorts with a tank top underneath and Birkenstock sandals.

As she organized her belongings between the back of the Durango and inside the Airstream, she thought about the dinner with Lillie after harvest. It was exactly what she needed after her heartbreaking conversation with Zach. Lillie knew heartbreak well, as she had returned from France pregnant and without Paul earlier last year. Kate admired how strong she had to be to get through that time of uncertainty. With the loss of their mother, they really only had each other to lean on at that time. Well, besides Caroline.

Yet, unbelievably, Paul came after Lillie and proposed. Their love overcame the miscommunication and hurt, and they married at Winsome Winery in an exquisitely beautiful ceremony.

Kate tucked a stray hair into her bandana as she watched the black grackles screeching at each other as they flit around the roofs of RVs across the way.

She realized that their extended family had

grown in the past year, mostly around Zach and the winery. With Dennis taking a semi-paternal role in their lives, and the rest of the community embracing Lillie and Paul at the tasting room, Kate felt good about heading out, that she wasn't leaving her sister alone.

There was a nagging in the back of her mind, and a tugging at her heart, though. Without Zach, she wasn't sure how she fit into this community now. Would she be as welcome when she returned? Or was this a chapter of her life that was ending?

Kate brushed away the thought as she remembered what Lillie had said: *Sis, you've done this all on your own. You're an amazing writer, and you deserve the recognition. If there's something here for you, it will be here when you get back.*

Kate took a deep breath and let it out, hoping that Lillie was right.

She was maneuvering the small storage compartments, pulling some things out and placing the items she'd need most up front, shoving the rest in back when a vehicle pulled up to her campsite.

She poked her head out to see Zach step out, and her breath hitched.

They hadn't spoken since that conversation on the porch earlier that week. There had been nothing more to say. He had told her his truth, that he wanted more from their relationship, and that he couldn't do long distance for a year. Once he had explained what led to his own divorce, she finally understood.

Kate gulped hard and watched him come around his Range Rover and step towards her. His tall, familiar frame made her instantly want to run into his arms, but she stood firm.

"Kate. I'm glad I caught you before you left," he said, coming closer to her.

"Zach, I don't think there's anything else to say. You made yourself perfectly clear the other day, and I respect that," Kate said.

"I know you need to leave, but please, sit with me for just a minute." He motioned her to the picnic bench at her campsite.

They sat down side by side, and Kate felt all kinds of confusing emotions—longing to touch him, wanting to push him away.

He sat looking at her Airstream, and then around the campsite. "You know, I don't remember the last time I came to visit you."

Kate thought about that, and realized he was right. She was always going into town to meet him.

"Well, the full-size bed is a bit small for both of us," she said.

"No, I mean, it's sort of always been on my terms, right?"

She looked at him thoughtfully, starting to realize that he was correct.

"It was all about my tasting room, my wine, my relationship with Chloe..." He trailed off and gently put his hand on top of hers. The warmth shot straight to Kate's heart.

"Well, I guess so," Kate said. "Maybe that's why I was so insistent on living separately and staying here. I think after my all-consuming marriage, and then losing everything, I just couldn't risk losing myself again in another relationship." She paused and looked up at him. "I don't know if I can be that girl again. The one who makes her world revolve around a man."

He squeezed her hand. "I don't want you to do that either. I realize that I've been a bit selfish, thinking that you needed to fit into my world." He cleared his throat. "I'm sorry about that. Really."

Kate took him to heart, and they sat for a while letting it all soak in. The love between them felt so palpable, and yet unattainable.

"So, what's going to happen? Will we be friends still?" Kate asked, her voice thin.

"Absolutely." He turned towards her, grabbing both hands. "Kate, I will always love you. Maybe I can't do a long-distance relationship, but I will always be here for you, and be your friend."

"Really?" she half-croaked.

"Scouts honor." He crossed his heart, breaking the intensity for a moment.

"Good. Because I would hate to lose you after everything we went through to find each other. And everything we have gone through since!" She half-smiled. "You're family to me."

"That will never change."

He pulled her into him, and they held each other crushingly close. Kate could feel his heartbeat strong against her chest, and she breathed his scent deep one last time.

"Listen, please be safe out there, and call me if you need anything." He pulled away from her and stood up. "Even if just to talk."

"Okay. I will," Kate said and stood up as he made his way back to the driver's side of his car.

They held each other's gaze for a moment, and then he got in and slowly drove off.

Kate watched a lone hawk circling lazily in the sky above, and she swallowed her sadness. Somehow, knowing they would still be connected in some way eased the pain a bit.

Just like that hawk, Kate knew her solo adventures were about to begin again, and she felt as ready as she would ever be.

Letter from the Author

Hello Readers!

It's lovely to be back with you again on the Texas wine trail. It took me a bit longer to get this one out, but hopefully it was worth the wait. It was great fun to write my first "mystery", and I also loved digging deeper into the characters while introducing you to new places.

As always, please share with others, and come visit Fredericksburg and the Hill Country of Texas. The wineries, and locally-owned businesses greatly appreciate it. Be sure to tell them you read about them in this book!

I'm happy to join in person and virtual book clubs, so be sure to reach out to me on either social media or through my website!

Warmest regards,
Heather & Dotty

Locations visited on the

Texas Wine Trail

Adega Vinho
Stonewall, TX
https://adegavinho.com

Alla Campagna
Fredericksburg, TX
https://www.allacampagnafbg.com

Arch Ray Resort & Winery
Fredericksburg, TX
https://archrayresort.com

Fredericksburg Trade Days
Fredericksburg, TX
http://www.fbgtradedays.com

Jack's Chophouse
Fredericksburg, TX
https://jackssteaks.com

Slate Theory Winery
Fredericksburg, TX
https://www.slatetheory.com

Speakeasy at Salvation Spirits
Fredericksburg, TX
https://www.salvationspeakeasy.com

Stone House Vineyard
Spicewood, TX
https://stonehousevineyard.com

Sunday Supply
Fredericksburg, TX
https://www.sundaysupplytx.com

Sunset Grill
Fredericksburg, TX
https://www.sunsetgrillfbgtx.com

⇉ Acknowledgements ⇇

I'm so lucky to have such a great core team of people who help me, and they have been the same for all three books in the Texas Wine Trail Series so far!

Thank you, Dan & the team at NYBookEditors. Megan McKeever, I am forever digging deeper for you and this time is no different. Truly, it would not be the same without your guidance and support. Robert J., you helped me fine-tune my dialogue and I greatly appreciate your thorough copy-edits.

Thank you, Christine, my book cover guru!

Every time I wonder how you will incorporate a design that will flow with the previous covers, and you always nail it on the first go-around! Your keen eye and attention to detail always makes the interior layout one of the best on the market!

Thank you, Victoria, for your beautifully hand-drawn illustrations–they add the perfect touch for each chapter!

Thank you, Deanna, Mike, and the team at Longhorn Cellars Winery for my "research" hand-harvesting merlot grapes (and, for the delicious wine!).

Thank you Daphne & Don Lusk for your encouragement and keeping the wine flowing in Waco. Deborah Monlux for coming out during the eclipse & your friendship and support over the years. Cindy Davie for always being my "first" reader! Thanks to all of my friends who encourage me to continue to follow my dreams and passions wherever they may lead!

Of course, I couldn't do all this without my partner-in-crime, one-of-a-kind, gorgeously opinionated pup, Dotty. She is my entire heart.

Finally, but certainly not least, to my readers: I am SO very grateful that you have pushed me to write another book in this series. Your messages on social media were timely and helped give me the courage and endurance to get this book finished. Thank you!

Happy wine trails!

CACTUS CHRISTMAS

A TEXAS WINE TRAIL SERIES

⇉ BOOK 1 ⇇

Heather Renée May

ORDER TODAY!

Find out where you can order online, or pick up signed copies at participating wineries on the Texas wine trail!

www.heatherreneemay.com

CACTUS WEDDING

A TEXAS WINE TRAIL SERIES

⇒ BOOK 2 ⇐

Heather Renée May

ORDER TODAY!

Sign up today for email notifications for book tour events, author meet & greets, and much more!

www.heatherreneemay.com

About the Author

Heather Renée May is a lover of music, dogs, cheese, and wine, not necessarily in that order. She is a lead software engineer, podcast host, and musician. She travels around in her RV with her adorable bestie, Dotty. You can find out more on her website: www.heatherreneemay.com